DOMINANT F

Clandestine Affairs 4

Zara Chase

MENAGE EVERLASTING

Siren Publishing, Inc.
www.SirenPublishing.com

A SIREN PUBLISHING BOOK
IMPRINT: Ménage Everlasting

DOMINANT FORCE
Copyright © 2014 by Zara Chase

ISBN: 978-1-62741-514-9

First Printing: July 2014

Cover design by Les Byerley
All art and logo copyright © 2014 by Siren Publishing, Inc.

Printed in the U.S.A.

PUBLISHER
Siren Publishing, Inc.
www.SirenPublishing.com

DOMINANT FORCE

Clandestine Affairs 4

ZARA CHASE
Copyright © 2014

Chapter One

Raoul dove into the frigid water and swam beneath it until his lungs felt ready to burst. *Ah shit, I can't do this.* His head broke the surface, and he shook his hair back from his eyes and trod water as he fed his screaming lungs with fresh Wyoming air. Zeke dove in at the same time as Raoul, but surfaced a good hundred feet farther ahead and almost a minute after Raoul ran out of air. Sometimes Raoul thought his buddy was more than just Native American—he was frigging Superman. Nothing seemed to faze him.

"You're getting soft in your old age," Zeke yelled, grinning.

Raoul flipped him off and swam away. "We can't all be fucking amphibians," he said. "You were always better at this shit than me."

"You ain't too bad." Zeke rolled onto his back and floated, staring up at the crystal clear sky. "For an old guy."

"Fuck you."

"You sure need to fuck someone. Your dick will fall off from lack of use if you carry on the way you're going."

Zeke turned almost soundlessly and swam up to join Raoul, his crawl seemingly effortless as he cut through the water, making barely a ripple. The two men swam hard to the end of the lake. It took them five minutes to get there. Instead of resting, they flipped around and swam straight back again. A cold lake that would have seen even the strongest of swimmers struggling was no big deal for Raoul and Zeke. Neither of them was breathing particularly hard when they reached their starting point and hauled themselves out. Both of them had swum in the buff. There was no one around to see them. Not that they would have given a shit if there was. This was private land—their land—so anyone trespassing got what they deserved.

"Good thing I slowed down, old man, and let you keep up with me," Zeke said, reaching for his towel.

Raoul did the same thing, feeling refreshed and invigorated, but still unable to shake off the restlessness that had gripped him for some weeks now. Running this horse ranch, and the Clandestine Affairs agency, ought to be enough for him—one activity fed his love of the outdoors, the other sated his need to right just a few of the world's wrongs.

Raoul and Zeke had seen more than their fair share of excitement—make that human misery—during their tours of duty as elite Special Forces Green Berets. They were still doing good through their investigation agency, only now it was on Raoul's terms. He got to dispense his own form of justice, without reference to Uncle Sam's rules and regulations, or the politically correct bullshit that had taken over the modern world. The irony was, the military sometimes came knocking at Raoul's door, wanting him to clean up its own messes. Deniability.

"You just keep telling yourself that, if it makes you feel better," Raoul said, slapping his buddy's rock-hard shoulder as they made their way back to the house.

Even so, he knew Zeke had a point, and that he was worried about Raoul. The two of them used to be all action, living, working, and especially playing hard. They went for the same type of women, and enjoyed sharing them. It had been a while since Raoul had felt like doing that, and hell if he knew why. In spite of the fact that he kept himself so busy, recently it hadn't felt like enough. Perhaps Zeke was right, and it was time for him to return to the real world.

Both men showered, after which Raoul figured Zeke would disappear into the horse barn. He had a real way with horses, but then Zeke had a real way with just about everything he touched, including women. Especially women. They flocked to him in droves, attracted by his tough image and swarthy good looks. Horses virtually sang to him, and it never took him long to have even the most spirited equine dancing to his tune.

Raoul sighed as he headed for his state-of-the-art office, from which he kept on top of his operatives' activities twenty-four-seven. He accessed his e-mail, but found nothing interesting to detain him there. He placed a couple of calls, then headed for the kitchen and flipped on the kettle. Caffeine was definitely on his immediate agenda, and he had just finished grinding the beans when his phone rang.

"Washington," he said curtly, pressing the speaker phone button as he continued to assemble the coffee.

"Mr. Washington." The woman's voice on the other end of the phone was little more than a whisper. A terrified whisper.

"Yeah, what can I do for you?" Raoul knew when a person was in trouble and, coffee abandoned, he gave the woman his full attention. Zeke moving silently into the room behind him, presumably because his sixth sense had told him they had a situation—just like it always seemed to.

"My name's Anais Harrison. My husband Gary was in SOCOM."

Raoul exchanged a glance with Zeke as he opened a database on his computer he probably wasn't supposed to have access to. Make that definitely wasn't supposed to. SOCOM was the US Special Operations Command, with headquarters in Florida. It was a joint forces command manned by elite personnel who were called in to cover covert and clandestine operations—anything from direct action and special recon to counter-terrorism and counter-narcotics.

"Okay," Raoul said, searching his database for the name Harrison. "You say 'was.'"

"He went missing in action two years ago. No one can tell me what happened, so I've been trying to find out for myself. Since I started asking questions, I've been threatened verbally, and my car was vandalized. I ignored the threats so far, but when I tried to go home just now, the door to my apartment was hanging off its hinges."

"Did you go in?"

"Hell, no! I hightailed it for my car before I was seen."

"You did the right thing." Raoul flexed his brows at Zeke. "Where are you now? Tell me you're not on your cell phone."

"No, I've watched enough detective programs to know I can be traced through it. I'm on a payphone in a strip mall outside St. Pete Beach." Her voice trembled. "I'm real scared, Mr. Washington. My friend Eloise gave me your number a while back when Gary went missing. She said you helped her and that you would probably help me if I ever needed it." She paused. "I didn't want to bother you then, but I could sure use your help now."

Raoul thought quickly. Oh yeah, he remembered Eloise. She was getting seven shades of shit beaten out of her by her pilot husband. He was such a hot shot that no one believed he could possibly do such a thing, and so no one did anything to help her. No one except Raoul's people, that is. Eloise was now free of domestic abuse and her husband wouldn't be hitting any more women for a long time. It explained how Anais had gotten his number. It wasn't in the phone book, and he was careful who he gave it to. Eloise shouldn't have passed it on, but something about the desperation in Anais's voice made him glad she had. He was a sucker for a woman in need.

Zeke scrolled through the database and pointed to an entry for Sergeant First Class Gary Harrison, listed as MIA January two years previously. So far the woman checked out.

"Can you give me the address where you are now?" Raoul asked.

"Yes." Anais reeled it off.

"Okay, stay where you are, Anais." Raoul came to a decision he didn't really need to think about. "I'll see who I have down there and get someone to come and help you out. I'll call you right back."

"Thank you." She sounded on the verge of hysteria. "Please hurry."

"I'm on it."

"Sounds like the perfect job for Griffin and Kyler," Zeke said as soon as Raoul hung up. "They were both SOCOM before they saw the light and got out."

"Yeah, that's right. Pull me up their number."

Chapter Two

Hunter Griffin had just docked their thirty-eight-foot Boston Whaler fishing boat when his cell phone rang. He stepped onto the dock where his buddy, Lewis Kyler, was making the lines secure and setting up the shore power. Hunter checked the phone's display.

"It's Raoul," he told Lewis. "Wonder what's up."

"A job hopefully," Lewis replied. "I'm fed up with doing nothing more exciting than taking punters fishing."

"Yeah, yeah." Hunter took the call. "Hey, Raoul, how's it going?"

"A damsel in distress down your way," Raoul replied. "I thought of you guys straight away. Sounds right up your street."

"Is she young and good looking?" Hunter grinned as Lewis, who immediately perked up. "We got a sale on this week for young and good looking."

"Can't say," Raoul replied. "But I do know she's scared shitless."

Hunter sobered as he listened to Raoul tell him what little he knew about the lady in question. "This is where she's at right now." Raoul reeled off an address. "She's waiting on you."

"Okay, I know where that is. Tell her to hang tight and we'll be right there. We drive a navy blue Dodge truck."

"Let me know what you need when you've spoken to her."

"Will do." Hunter cut the call. "Come on, buddy. I'll fill you in on the way."

The guys jogged to their truck and Hunter fired up the engine. It took them ten minutes to reach the strip mall, and all of thirty seconds to find the payphone. They stopped right next to it, and saw a tall, slim woman with thick chestnut hair piled on top of her head cowering in the booth. Lewis let out a slow, appreciative whistle.

"The day just got a whole lot better," he said.

"She ain't exactly making herself inconspicuous," Hunter replied, "but I guess she'd have trouble blending in with a crowd."

She looked up, her eyes round with fear, when the truck stopped beside her. Lewis opened his door, jumped out, and smiled at her.

"Hey, Anais," he said. "Raoul sent us."

She looked at him through enormous, frightened eyes, and exhaled. "Oh, thank God for that!"

"Come on, honey, jump in. I'm Lewis and this is Hunter. You're safe now."

"My car's over there," she said, pointing to an old Jeep.

"Give me the keys." Lewis held out his hand. "I'll deal with it, make sure we're not followed. You just go with Hunter."

"Hey," Hunter said as Anais, her entire body trembling, slid into the seat Lewis had just vacated. "Nice to meet you."

"Me too. Wish it could have been under different circumstances. Thanks for coming so quickly."

"Our pleasure. It's what we do."

"I can't go back to my place," she said. "I don't think it's safe."

"No, we'll take you to ours. We can talk there and try to figure this thing out. You did well not to use your cell. If people really are following you, they could get to you that way."

"Yes." She glanced out the window and must have seen Lewis going all over her Jeep with a wand. "What's he doing?"

"Looking to see if anyone's placed a tracking device on your car."

She gasped. "Who would go that far?"

Hunter shrugged. "You tell me."

Lewis held up a hand, grimaced, and after a moment during which he ducked out of sight, he climbed behind the wheel of Anais's car. Hunter chuckled, having a pretty good idea what he'd just done.

"He found one," he said.

The fear was back in her eyes. "You're kidding me."

"Afraid not." Hunter squeezed her trembling hand. "You really do seem to have upset some serious people, honey." He put the truck into gear and pulled out of the lot. "Let's get you out of here. Then we'll talk."

"While I was waiting for you, I'd almost persuaded myself I was reading more into this than is actually there. I'd managed to calm down a bit."

Hunter shot her an appraising glance. "I wouldn't have liked to see the way you were when you were upset."

She gave a nervous laugh. "Yeah, sorry, it's been a tough time."

"You don't need to apologize to me. I can't begin to imagine what you've been through."

Hunter turned onto a side road with Lewis directly behind him in Anais's car. He cast sideways glances at his passenger as he did so. She was probably five seven, with all that glorious chestnut hair, and leaf-green eyes cloudy with fear he would definitely go that extra mile to get rid of. Seeing those amazing eyes sparkling with pleasure would be a result worth fighting for, no question. She wasn't classically beautiful, but still a traffic-stopper. She exuded a sensuality she probably wasn't aware she possessed, along with a vulnerability and a certain air of determination that broke through her fear. Her slim body, with all those enticing curves, had already gotten him salivating, and Lewis would definitely want to know if the freckles dotted across the bridge of her nose were replicated on other parts of her body. *Whoa, don't go there. She's a client.*

"Here we are."

Hunter pulled into the driveway of their waterside townhouse and pushed the button on the truck's visor to open the garage door. Lewis drove her Jeep into the garage, too, and Hunter closed the door again.

"Come on, babe, let's get you inside."

"Oh, this is nice." She glanced through the full-length windows in the living area that looked out directly onto the intracoastal waterway.

Sunshine dappled the water a dozen different shades of turquoise. A small motor boat was moored on their private dock, a pelican sitting in stately splendor on its guard rail. "Do you both live here?"

"Not in the way you're thinking," Lewis replied. "But yeah, we live and work together."

"You're ex-military?"

"Yep." It was Hunter who answered her. "We're ex-SOCOM, like your husband, so that's probably why Raoul thought we were the right people to help you."

"I really appreciate it. I must have inconvenienced you."

"We live to serve." Lewis winked at her as he led her to a settee. "Okay, let's get our priorities straight. It's almost the cocktail hour." He grinned. "Well, it has to be somewhere in the world. Anyway, this is an emergency and you look like you could use a drink. What can I get you?"

"Got any gin?"

It was Hunter's turn to grin. "We have tonic, too."

"Yes, please."

Lewis poured her a generous measure of gin, but was stinting with the tonic. He opened beers for himself and Hunter and the guys took up seats of the settee directly opposite hers. They watched her as she took a healthy sip of her drink, and savored it. Almost immediately Hunter sensed some of the tension drain out of her.

"Okay, babe," he said, crossing one ankle over his opposite thigh. "Start at the beginning. Tell us everything you know about your husband's disappearance. Then we need to know about all the odd stuff that's happened to you since you started asking questions."

* * * *

Anais took a moment to marshal her thoughts. That was no easy task when surrounded by two such virile males oozing machismo and excess testosterone. Just looking at them did weird things to her head.

Or perhaps that was just the gin. Somehow she doubted it. It wasn't every day a girl got such a treat. These guys weren't just tough and capable, they were every woman's fantasy, and then some. Anais excused her wayward thoughts by reminding herself she had been a man-free zone since Gary went AWOL. That didn't mean she was dead, or blind, which also meant it was impossible for her not to appreciate the view.

All taut muscle, tightly controlled strength and lithe coordination, Anais was finding it increasingly difficult not to gawp at them like a love-struck teen. Less than an hour ago she was frightened half out of her wits, now she was getting hot under the collar, and all points south of it, for very different reasons. Jeez!

Hunter kept his long brown hair held back in a ponytail. His strong jaw was covered in a day's worth of stubble and his compelling deep brown eyes that appeared to miss little. Just being in the same room with him made her feel safe—and other emotions that had no place in their relationship. Lewis, with lighter brown hair and sea blue eyes, was all wide shoulders and possessed a lazy, mercurial charm that immediately reassured. But there was a downside to every situation, and being confronted by decadent Greek gods with hard unyielding bodies and intoxicating animal magnetism definitely didn't do much for her cognitive powers.

"Gary was regular army," she said, resorting to another quick slug of gin to keep her mind where it was supposed to be. "A tactical shooter, he could hit anything from two hundred paces with the wind in the wrong direction. We met as kids in Tennessee, he had been hunting almost as long as he could walk, and guns were second nature to him."

"He was recommended for SOCOM because of his skills with a gun?" Hunter asked.

"Yes, and he loved it. Loved being part of the elite. Took to it like a kiddie to a sandpit."

"So you moved to Florida," Lewis said. "Did you live on base?"

"Yes."

"And," Hunter prompted when she said nothing more.

She shrugged. "There's not much more to say about it. Some wives take to military life, some don't. I'm one that didn't. I would have preferred to live off base. I had no kids, and not much in common with the other wives, but Gary was away a lot of missions and said he felt happier knowing I had people around me."

"Do you work?" Lewis asked.

"Yes, I'm a freelance editor. I do some work for a publishing house, and a lot more for authors who want to self-publish."

"So there was no getting away to the office for you," Hunter said.

"No, that was part of the problem."

"How were things with you and Gary?" Hunter asked. "I'm sorry if that sounds personal, but I need to build up a picture of your background. You implied you were childhood sweethearts—"

"Yes, he's the only man I've ever known."

She noticed the guys share a glance, telling herself she had no reason to feel defensive just because she had stuck to her wedding vows. They probably thought she was hopelessly naïve, but she couldn't help the way she was.

"So you were happy, I take it." She nodded in response to Hunter's assumption. "Why no kids, if you don't mind me asking?"

"I wanted them, but Gary only had another couple of years to go in the army. He wasn't going to sign on for more. He wanted to wait until he was out and we could be together all the time. He said he wanted to be a hands-on father, but I also think he was worried something might happen to him and didn't want to leave me alone literally holding the baby." She blinked back tears. "As it happens, he was right."

"Tell us what happened." Lewis sent her a smile that melted her insides. She had only known them for half an hour but already felt she could say absolutely anything to them. "All we know is that he's been classified missing in action. We don't want to upset you, darlin', but if we're going to help you, we need to know everything."

"It's okay. It's been two years, and I've spoken about it a lot."

"I assume he was on a mission," Hunter said.

His question barely registered with Anais. He still had one ankle hitched over his opposite thigh, giving her a clear view of the worn denim covering his groin and the impressive bulge pressing against his zipper. She moistened her lips, finding it hard to drag her eyes away. Only when she noticed both guys looking at her with knowing glances did she blush and reapply her attention to her drink.

"No, about six months before he went missing, he was taken off active service."

"What!" Both guys sat upright, which meant both of Hunter's feet hit the floor and she lost the view she had been fixating on. "Why was that?" he asked.

She shrugged. "Gary didn't know, or wouldn't tell me, but he was furious about it. I'd never seen him in such a mood before. I couldn't get through to him. He told me he thought it might have been because he'd made it clear he wasn't signing on again."

"They put him on training duties?" Lewis asked. "If he was such a good shot, I'm guessing that's what happened."

"Right, and he hated it. I was glad because, stupidly, I thought now he wasn't being assigned overseas, he would be safe. Besides, we would be together all the time, and I looked forward to that, but it was difficult. Gary was permanently angry, and our relationship suffered. Like I said before, I couldn't get through to him. He always used to talk to me about anything and everything. Once he came off active duties, he withdrew into himself, started to drink more, and…well, he wasn't the man I'd married."

"How did he go missing if he was on instructor duties?" Lewis asked.

"That's what I've wanted to know for the past two years." She shrugged. "But if anyone knows, they're not telling. All I do know is that he was an instructor on a two-day survival course for a bunch of recruits. You know the sort of stuff. They're left in one location, and have to make their way back to wherever the instructors are in a given amount of time. They live off the land, and all that. Gary saw them off, and checked on them unannounced at various points on the course, but never appeared at the final rendezvous. A massive search was launched for him, but he was never found." Fresh tears threatened, but Anais blinked them away. "His pack was found, so too was his precious rifle, with blood of the stock. His blood group. But Gary disappeared without trace."

"I don't mean to upset you, babe," Hunter said. "But could he not just have done a runner?"

"Deserted, you mean?" Hunter and Lewis both nodded. "No, he would never do that. Despite hating being sidelined, Gary still loved everything about the military. Anyway, he would never have left me. Our relationship was going through a bad patch, but it was still solid."

"Then why wasn't his body found? Where did this exercise take place?"

"The Everglades," she said bleakly.

"Ah."

"Precisely. There are a thousand places a man could disappear in that hostile territory and never be found. Even someone as experienced as Gary, or that's what the Department of Defense kept telling me every time I asked what they were doing to find him."

"Did all the recruits make the rendezvous unscathed?"

"Yes, that's what is so odd about it." Anais frowned as she shifted her position and rested her elbow on the back cushion of the couch. She kicked off her sandals and tucked one foot beneath her butt. "At the time I was too upset to ask questions. I simply moved off the base, and took a rented apartment here on the beach. But I couldn't seem to move on with my life. As I got over my initial grief, I started to ask myself questions. I mean, how would you feel if you didn't even know whether the love or your life was dead or alive? Well, obviously

I know he's dead, otherwise he would have found his way out of the Everglades long before now. Surviving off the land is what Gary does…did. But I need to know what happened. I couldn't bury him, all I could do was have a memorial service. No, make that the military kinda forced me into having one, and I went along with it because I thought it might give me closure." She shook her head. "It didn't."

"They do like everything neat and tidy," Lewis said with a sympathetic smile. "You shouldn't have let them bully you, but I understand why you did. You were hurting and vulnerable."

"I felt like it wasn't happening to me. I was numb. I mean, I always knew Gary might not come back from one of his assignments abroad. All military wives are programmed that way. But he was a frigging instructor stateside, for God's sake. I thought he was safe." She impatiently brushed away tears with the back of her hand. "I absolutely didn't see that one coming, and still need that elusive closure." He steady gaze encompassed them both. "I need answers, gentlemen. Something isn't right about all this. I've been thinking that for a while, and after what happened today, I'm absolutely sure of it."

"Sounds as though you have reason to be." Hunter stood up, took her empty glass from her hand and refilled it. "Raoul said you were pretty shaken up when you rang him. Presumably you started asking awkward questions about Gary and were warned off. What happened?"

"I applied to the Department of Defense. I wanted to see their files into the investigation. They said it was classified."

"They would." Lewis rolled his eyes. "So what did you do next?"

"I went to his CO, but got stonewalled there, too. It was infuriating. He almost patted me on the head and told me not to worry my pretty little head about it. Damned dinosaur! I thought that sort of patronizing attitude went out years ago. Seems I was wrong."

"And I'm betting the more you got told *no* the more suspicious you became and the more determined you were to get answers," Hunter said, passing a fresh beer to Lewis.

"Right. There's a chat room military wives hang out in. Nothing classified, of course. Just women in the same situation giving one another support. I got on there, talking about Gary's disappearance, asking if any of their husbands had served with him, stuff like that. That earned me a visit from military police, telling me politely but firmly to leave it alone."

"Who came to see you?" Hunter asked.

"A Major Dixon. He actually listened to me and told me the military were still looking into Gary's disappearance. He actually made me feel better. It was like he took my concerns seriously, but he told me I had to leave it be and let them do their job. He'd get back to me if he found anything solid. Needless to say, I've not heard from him again."

"The wheels of military justice turn slowly," Lewis said.

"Yeah, but someone like Dixon taking the time to talk to me solidified my belief that something was off. I started out just wanting to know what they knew. I didn't really think there was anything sinister. The Everglades *are* dangerous. Even someone as experienced as Gary might have gotten careless, which is all it would have taken. Only when they refused to tell me anything did I think there might be a cover-up, and I was more determined than ever to get to the truth." She flashed a mischievous smile. "So, I started blogging about my suspicions. I mean, the military can stop me talking to other wives, and I did stop because I didn't want to drop them in it, but there's diddly-squat they can do about my personal blog."

"But they did?" Lewis suggested.

"Someone did. I started getting threatening phone calls. Some creep saying he knew where I lived, and knew where my aged mother lives, too. He even quoted her address. It made my skin crawl, but I was damned if I'd give in to bullies. I contacted the local paper, tried to get them interested, recorded all my phone calls, stuff like that. But the paper wouldn't do much. They said if I found anything out they would look at it, but couldn't print unsubstantiated theories from a grieving widow for fear of coming across as unpatriotic."

"Wusses," Lewis said, scowling.

"Just after that my car was vandalized. Then, today, I got back to my apartment. The front door was off its hinges, like someone had kicked it in and wanted me to know it. They certainly weren't subtle about it." She shrugged, trying to appear casual, even though that was the last way she felt. "Well, that's when I got the message. There's a cover-up of some sort going on, and they don't want me poking about in it. If they planted a tracking device on my car, then it proves it." She glanced at Lewis. "What did you do with it, by the way?"

Lewis grinned. "Right now, the people who planted it will be tracking the Lexus that was parked next to you in that lot."

"So they will think I found it and am fighting back."

"Probably," Hunter agreed. "But they can't get to you, babe, not here."

"I can't stay here indefinitely."

"We'll get to that in a minute."

"Okay." She sipped at her new drink. "I'll admit that going home right now is a scary prospect. They intended to frighten me and did a damned good job of it by invading my personal space."

She shuddered, and Hunter reached across to touch her hand. "Were they still inside?"

"I don't know," Anais replied, surprised that the mere touch of Hunter's hand should have such a profound, albeit reassuring, effect on her. "I hightailed it out of there, found that payphone and called Raoul. Thank God Eloise had given me his number and I had it in my purse."

"So, what do you need from us, babe?" Hunter asked.

She fixed them both with a determined gaze. "I want you to help me find out what happened to my husband."

Chapter Three

"We can help you with that." Hunter sent their client a reassuring smile, reminding himself for the tenth time at least that she *was* a client, and therefore off limits. "But like I said earlier, you can't go back to your apartment. Someone's got it in for you."

"I need some things. My laptop, some clothes."

"Lewis will go back there, fix your door and pick up anything you need."

"I'll come, too. I—"

"No, I don't want you going, just in case the place is being watched."

Her eyes widened. "You think someone will be watching by apartment?"

"Until we know who's behind all this, I've no way of knowing, but I don't plan on taking any chances. Lewis can go in looking like a locksmith."

"You can do the door yourself?"

"Sure." Lewis winked at her. "You have no idea how many talents I possess."

"Modesty not being one of them," Hunter added, smirking.

"Unlike you, buddy, I have nothing to be modest about."

She looked bewildered by their banter. "Do you think the military broke into my apartment?" she asked. "Am I stirring things up that much?"

"The military don't want you poking about, but that might just be because they're being their usual paranoid selves," Hunter replied.

"And it doesn't look good on the recruiting posters if they lose an experienced instructor in the Everglades," Lewis added, a cynical twist to his lips.

"So, who...my apartment, my vandalized car, the tracker—"

Hunter shrugged. "That, darlin', is what we aim to find out."

"But I still don't understand." Hunter was surprised by the strength of his desire to wipe the bewildered frown from her adorable brow. "Why would anyone other than the military care?"

"Another good question." Lewis sent her one of his killer smiles, causing her to blush. "Do you have access to his e-mail account?"

"Yes, but there's nothing interesting there. He wasn't a great one for technology. Just the odd communication between him and pals, making dates to go fishing, stuff like that."

"What about his cell phone?"

Her expression closed down. "He had it with him."

"We'll need to look at his phone records, see if any numbers jump out at us," Hunter said.

"Okay, but the military already did."

Hunter shared a glance with Lewis, both probably thinking the same thing. If a guy went missing on a routine training exercise, why did they need to examine his phone records? This got weirder by the minute. The more they found out, the more it smelled like a cover-up.

"Do you know where he was stationed before being reassigned to training duties?"

"No." She shook her head. "He wasn't allowed to tell me, and I'd long since learned not to ask. Seeing him come back in one piece was enough for me." Her faraway expression told Hunter she had regressed to the past. "Those were the best times. He was always stoked after doing whatever it was he'd been sent away to do. That all changed when his life offered nothing more taxing than a training exercise. I couldn't reach him after that. He was like a stranger."

Lewis finished his beer and stood up. "Okay, sweetheart, give me your apartment address and an idea of what you need me to bring back here."

Hunter watched Lewis working his charm on Anais. She visibly relaxed beneath the heat of his full-wattage smile as she gave him a verbal list of the things she needed. She was already a different creature from the frightened female they had collected from that pay phone only an hour or so ago. He got the impression she had learned to be self-sufficient—most military wives had to be—and didn't often let anything scare her. Having their backing had already seen a revival of her spirit. That was good, just so long as she didn't try and go off some place on her own.

Her *perfect* husband had been into something he couldn't control, that much was already obvious to Hunter, and probably to Lewis as well, but Anais wasn't ready to hear it yet. Whatever Gary had going, he'd pissed off the wrong people and paid a heavy price for it. He had died somewhere in the vast expanse of the Everglades and the chances of finding his body were practically nil. The sorts of people he had gone up against had put a tracker on a woman's car and vandalized her apartment, so were not to be messed with. Well, not without the sort of help Hunter and Lewis specialized in.

Gripped by a quite violent desire to keep Anais safe, Hunter already knew this was more than just another assignment. There was something about Anais that had gotten under his skin. Okay, so she was a classy babe, but he and Lewis had a ready supply of those coming on to them all the time and they had learned to be selective. He'd been impressed when Anais told them Gary was the only man she had ever known. She seemed to think it was something to be ashamed of, rather than a refreshing change.

She and the saintly Gary had been childhood sweethearts, and she had stuck to her wedding vows. Obviously, that situation must have changed over the past two years. She was a sensual woman with personal needs, just like everyone. Hunter scowled, not wanting to think about the faceless men who must have queued up to comfort her, with the ultimate intention of getting inside her panties.

That was what Hunter wanted to do as well, rather desperately as it happened, but it wouldn't, well…happen. Not yet at any rate. He would help her figure out what had happened to Gary, and then see what developed. He didn't even have to look at Lewis to know he felt the same way. There was already a buzz in the atmosphere between the three of them. Persuading a widow with virtually no experience of men into a ménage wasn't something to be rushed, and ménages were where it was at from his and Lewis's perspective.

"Okay, I think I'm set." Lewis winked at Anais as he picked up the keys to the truck and headed for the internal door to the garage. "I'll swing by the hardware store and pick up a new lock, then get the stuff you need, babe. Play nice without me, guys."

"I'll start dinner," Hunter said.

"Good plan."

It was quiet when Lewis left them, the atmosphere fuelled with expectancy, or was that just wishful thinking on Hunter's part? He glanced at Anais, who had resumed her seat. She seemed embarrassed to be alone with him, and looked everywhere except in his direction. Hunted didn't want her to feel uncomfortable, and blamed himself for allowing sexual tension to mess with his mind. He felt guilty for having lascivious thoughts about a woman still grieving for her lost husband but, shit, life was for the living, and just looking at Anais gave him a raging hard-on. Nothing he could do about that.

"You want me to show you the guest room?" he asked.

"Oh yes, if you don't mind."

She placed her glass aside and stood up. Hunter headed for the stairs, acutely aware of the floral fragrance that clung to her and the soft sound of her breathing as she followed behind him. He threw open the door to the guest room. It housed a queen-sized bed and light oak furniture. The drapes were drawn back and the view from this room, just like all the others in the house, looked directly onto the water.

"There's a bath through there," he said, pointing to the door.

"Thanks, this is luxury. Are you sure I won't be in the way?"

Oh, you will be, sweetheart, but not for the reasons you suppose. "Not at all."

"I, err...well, this is a bit embarrassing, but obviously I need to pay you."

"Don't worry about it. If we get results, then we can talk money."

"But you can't work for nothing."

"That's up to Raoul. Sometimes the military employ us, and we charge them top dollar."

Anais's smile lit up her entire face. Shit, what was she doing to him? Tight jeans clung to long, slender legs and a neat ass he'd give a month's pay to spank. A skimpy tank top sculpted her tits. He could see her pert nipples through the lacy bra that supported them, and the sight was slowly driving him out of his mind. How the fuck was he supposed to function when he appeared to have a near-permanent erection each time he so much as looked at her?

"That seems only fair," she said, "but I still think I should pay you. I did okay when Gary was lost. The military pay me a pension, and I earn a good wage with my editing."

"But without a body I guess you can't claim on life insurance."

"That's true, but not why I want to find out what happened."

"Hey, I wasn't suggesting it was." Hunter held up both hands. "I know you need answers for your own peace of mind."

"Yes, I do."

There was an awkward pause. "Look, I'll leave you to get settled, and go down to start dinner."

She smiled again. *Don't do that! You have no idea what that smile does to me.* Well, she'd soon get a pretty damned good idea if she glanced down.

"There's nothing to settle until Lewis comes back with my stuff. I'll come and help in the kitchen if you could use some company. I like cooking."

The corners of his mouth turned up. "Your company's welcome any time."

* * * *

Was he flirting with her? Lewis had been earlier, no question, but Hunter was harder to read. He had made her feel welcome, and secure, but she still wasn't sure how he really felt about her invading his personal space. He seemed like a private person who didn't give much away about himself. Her staying here seemed a bit above and beyond, but he was right to say she couldn't go back to her apartment until they found some answers. The only alternative was a hotel, and that thought didn't appeal, so she'd try it here for a day or two and see how it went.

At least the guys had backed her theory that something was off about Gary's disappearance. They were right. The military worked by a strict code of rules, and would never stoop to intimidation. So who the hell would? She trusted these two to help her find out. She didn't know them, but they made her feel cherished in a way she hadn't known since Gary was taken off active duty and his entire attitude toward her had changed.

Hunter Griffin was a real enigma—a mixture of machismo, intelligence, hunky good looks…and cooking. Somehow that didn't quite fit. She asked him about it when they reached his state-of-the-art kitchen, just to break the tension she felt blossoming between them.

"I learned to cook when I was a kid," he said, pulling ingredients from the fridge. "It was that or starve to death. I'm the oldest of four, but feeding us didn't rate high on our mom's agenda. It was either junk food, or one of us had to learn to cook. I didn't want to turn into a lump of lard by filling myself with empty calories so I learned to cook." He shrugged. "Now I find it therapeutic."

"Well, it's a hell of a view to keep you focused while you cook." Anais glanced at Hunter rather than the water outside the kitchen window as she spoke. "What's on the menu tonight?"

"How does stuffed pork tenderloin, saffron rice, and salad sound?"

"Delicious. What can I do?"

"You take care of the rice, I'll stuff the meat and we can toss for who makes the salad."

"You've got yourself a deal."

They worked in companionable silence for a few minutes, Anais becoming increasingly aware of the strained atmosphere as she watched Hunter's long fingers stuffing the meat with dried apricots, pine nuts, and fresh herbs. It was sexual tension, she realized, wondering if it was in her imagination, or if Hunter felt it, too. If he did, he gave no sign.

"We need a decent red to go with this," he said, after he'd sealed the meat and placed it in the oven. He moved to a well-stocked wine cabinet, examined the labels, grunted when he found a bottle that met with his approval, and expertly removed the cork. "Food and drink rate together as the second most sensual pleasures on this earth, and it's a sin not to fully appreciate them."

She looked up at him, their gazes clashed, and then locked. Anais's physical reaction to her emotional turmoil was extreme. A tremor ran through her body as he devoured her with eyes that definitely wanted. She became conscious of liquid seeping from her pussy and sensation uncoiling deep in her gut.

"Am I supposed to ask what the winner is in the sensual stakes?" she asked, the desire she felt surging through her making her bold.

He sent her a sexy smile that made him look more handsome than ever, if exceedingly dangerous. Her mother's warning about never playing with fire ran through her mind. Given her current circumstances, getting burned might not be so bad. No pain, no gain.

"Baby, if you need to ask, your husband was doing something wrong."

His reference to Gary spoiled the mood, and they both appeared to realize it. Anais broke eye contact with him and rummaged in a drawer, searching for silverware.

"I'll set the table," she said.

"Sorry," he said at the same time.

She blinked. "For what?"

"Never mind. I've got the salad. You do the table."

"How do you plan to find out more about what happened to Gary?" she asked, desperate to break the taut silence that now prevailed.

"First off we need to find out where he was posted abroad."

"But the military won't say."

Hunter chuckled. "We won't ask them. Raoul has access to information you could only dream about. I'll have a word with him later. He'll soon have something for us."

"What can I do?"

"When Lewis gets back with your files, you'll have copies of Gary's cell phone accounts in them, right?"

"Yes, but—"

"We need to see what numbers he called regularly, follow them up, see where they lead, stuff like that. You can help by telling us who his friends were, who he was closest to in the squad. People often tell their buddies stuff they don't tell their wives."

"I spoke to a few people myself, but didn't come up with anything that helped."

"You did, babe, you just don't know it yet. If you were just pissing in the wind, people wouldn't be tracking your vehicle, or warning you off."

"I suppose."

Anais noticed a pretty scented candle in a holder sitting on the dresser in the dining nook. She reached for it and placed it in the center of the table, wondering at two guys having things like scented candles in their house. Presumably it was a present from one of their girlfriends. The thought brought her up short. She hadn't stopped to consider they might have significant others, but it stood to reason that two guys who looked the way they did must have women all over them. Jealousy surged through her. It was a unique feeling. Anais couldn't remember ever being jealous before in her entire life, and here she was getting all possessive over not one but two guys. She got herself back on track by remembering she was just another assignment to them.

Nothing more.

Looking more closely at their living space, she noticed a few other things. Throw pillows, healthy pot plants and other feminine touches.

"Look," she said. "I don't want to cramp your style. Like you said, I'll be perfectly safe here, so don't let me stop you doing whatever it is you normally do."

Hunter looked bewildered. "What do you mean?"

"Well, I'm sure you…you have women, and I—"

"You sure are pretty when you blush," he replied, chuckling.

"Oh, for goodness sake! I'm just trying to be thoughtful."

"We're cool. Lewis and I aren't seeing anyone right now." Anais frowned. He made it sound as though they shared. She had heard some people were like that, but had never thought to meet any of them. "We run a fishing charter business. That pretty much takes up our time."

"Oh, then you'll be out a lot of the time." God, she sounded so disappointed. So needy. *Get a grip, girl!*

"No, business is slow this time of year. We have a couple of employees who can take care of it while we're helping you out."

"In which case, I shall definitely pay you the going rate."

He moved as stealthily as a cat, making her jump when she felt his large body up close behind hers. The musky scent of his cologne and the even more enticingly smell of hot man mingled with the aroma of fresh herbs, making her senses reel.

"We're here to help," he said, his breath sending a tingle down the back of her neck as he spoke. "Money doesn't come into it."

"Why?" she asked, somehow forcing herself to move away from him. "Why would you want to work for nothing?"

He shrugged. "All of us who work for Raoul got pretty damned frustrated when we were in the service with all the red tape and rules and regulations. We saw so much shit go down, so many people get away with stuff they shouldn't, and there wasn't a fucking thing we could do about it because we're the good guys and we play fair. Raoul had more cause than most to get frustrated by it."

She leaned a hip against the work surface and found enough composure to look at him without blushing. That had to be progress. "Why is that?"

Hunter paused, as though he had said too much. Then he met her gaze and did a *what the hell* shrug. "He was married to a Palestinian lady who worked with the Americans, trying to broker peace. Some overambitious colonel sent her into a situation that Raoul and just about anyone else with two brain cells to rub together know would end in disaster." Hunter paused. "His wife finished up getting captured and killed. Raoul and Zeke went in after her, got caught and badly tortured, but managed to escape. I don't think Raoul has ever gotten over it, partly because there was fuck all he could do avenge his wife, and he wasn't allowed to separate that miserable colonel's head from his shoulders. The military take a dim view of that sort of thing."

"That's so sad," Anais said, feeling hot tears pricking the backs of her eyes.

"Yeah well, what we do now is Raoul's way of coping. He likes to think we might be able to save someone else going through what he went through. It's also his way of thumbing his nose at the powers that be."

"I don't think anyone could blame him for that."

"Right, we're all set here." He led the way back to the seating in the lounge. "Lewis should be back soon. Let's have a glass of that red while we wait for him."

Without waiting for her to answer, Hunter poured two glasses and handed one to her.

"Thank you."

"You're welcome."

Hunter seated himself across from her again, which disappointed Anais. She wouldn't mind having one of his muscular thighs pressed up against hers. Shit, she'd been living for too long with just a vibrator for company, obviously.

"That can't be your fishing charter boat," she said, pointing to the small, open craft moored to their dock, desperate for a neutral topic that steered well clear of her growing fixation with Hunter.

"No, we use that for getting around the waterways. It's faster in the winter when the roads are clogged with traffic, and most bars around here have docks for visiting boats."

"Ah yes, that makes sense I guess."

Anais was pleased when she heard the garage door open. Shortly thereafter Lewis appeared, toting a hold-all stuffed with her possessions.

"Honey, I'm home," he said. "What did I miss?"

Chapter Four

Hunter was glad of the interruption. An hour alone with Anais was enough for him to know that keeping his hands to himself was going to be a challenge, especially since he was getting responding vibes from her. He wondered if she knew she was giving them off. He couldn't remember the last time he'd crossed swords with a less predatory woman. It was refreshingly frustrating—heaven and hell combined. He and Lewis weren't in the habit of issuing women with open-ended invitations to invade their living space, especially ones who were off limits but what was done was done. They would just have to fall back on military discipline or, if that failed, take a bunch of cold showers.

"Hey, Lewis. Any problems?"

"I fixed the door up for you, babe." He handed Anais a new set of keys.

"Thank you," she replied. "How was it?"

"No lasting damage, but unfortunately your computer was taken."

"Shit!"

Hunter wasn't surprised. Even if this hadn't been a burglary, the perpetrators would want it to look like one.

"They probably want to find out what you know," he said. "I assume you kept a record of everything you'd learned about Gary's disappearance online?"

"Yep, but I'm not stupid."

She reached into her purse and waved a memory stick beneath their noses. Both men laughed.

"Clever girl," Lewis said. "Your paper files had been disrupted, and I couldn't find Gary's cell phone records."

"That's okay. I scanned them into the computer and they're on this stick, too. Not that they will do us much good, but I believe in being thorough." She paused. "Did they trash the place?"

Lewis hesitated. "It wasn't too bad. But they did leave you a message."

He pulled his cell phone from his pocket and showed them a picture he'd taken of the bathroom mirror, *Leave it Alone* scrawled across it in lipstick. Anais shuddered.

"Definitely not a burglary then."

"No. I took more pictures in case you want them for your insurers."

"Thanks, but if I do that I shall have to call the police, get a crime number and stuff, and I'm not sure I'm up for that. If it's just a case of replacing my laptop, I think I'll take the loss. It needed replacing anyway."

"That would probably be best." Hunter poured a glass of wine for Lewis, and then topped up his and Anais's glasses. "We have a spare laptop here you can use until you replace yours."

"That would be great, thanks."

"No problem. Any sign of watchers?" he asked Lewis.

"No one that I saw, but there was a bug." Anais gasped. "I left it where it was. They might think the one they left on your car fell off. It happens. But if the one in the apartment gets moved, too, they'll know you're on to them. All the time you don't go back there, it can't do any harm."

"I guess not, but I hate the thought of strangers being in my apartment, going through my things, invading my privacy." A combination of anger and fear flitted across her expression, severely testing Hunter's restraint, which had never been one of his strong points. If ever a woman needed consoling it was Anais, and Hunter only knew how to console a woman in one way, which was totally inappropriate in this situation. He shared a glance with Lewis, willing to bet his thoughts were running along similar lines, and shrugged.

"Look at it this way, babe," he said. "You must have discovered more about Gary's disappearance than you realized, and there's obviously more to it than you've been told. Otherwise why would these people bother to put the frighteners on you?"

"Yes, but I have no idea what." She sighed. "I'm left with more questions than answers."

"That's where we come in."

"I know." She blinked several times, as though trying to keep her emotions in check. "Don't take any notice of me. I'm cranky because I haven't been sleeping well."

"You'd be less than human if you weren't shaken," Hunter replied, winking at her. "But you're not in this alone anymore. We now know for sure that someone, somewhere has something to cover up, and we're just the people to find out what it is."

"Thanks for that. I'd be climbing the walls if I was still in this alone, and I do appreciate you putting your own business aside to help me." She stood up and reached for the bag of clothes Lewis had brought back for her. "Do I have time to freshen up before dinner?"

"Sure, take your time," Hunter replied.

"I've got that, babe." Lewis took the bag from her and headed for the stairs.

"I'm starting to feel spoiled," she said with a nervous little laugh.

Lewis came down again a short time later and threw himself into the seat Anais had just vacated.

"So, what do you make of it all?" he asked.

"I think we're in serious shit," Hunter replied.

"I take it you're not talking about the search for Anais's former nearest and dearest."

"You know damned well I'm not."

"Yeah, I hear you buddy." Lewis stretched both arms about his head and sighed. "But she's fragile, and she's a client. We can't make a move on her."

Hunter grunted. "You think I don't know that? All I know is having her living here but off-limits is gonna be a nightmare."

Lewis chuckled. "She's really got you thinking with your dick."

Hunter fixed his buddy with a dour look. "And you're not?"

"I hear you, partner." Lewis canted his head, his expression reflective. "Still and all, she's not in a good place right now. Besides, she's relatively innocent. She'd never play our games."

"Oh, I'm not so sure about that. I was getting vibes earlier. I don't think she realizes...well, what the fuck. It doesn't matter. You're right. We need to give her some space."

"So, we're agreed then, we keep it strictly business?"

"If we can." Hunter grunted, feeling restless, moody. "So, what's your take on her problems?"

"Either Gary fell into a swamp and got eaten by a reptile."

"Not likely, given he was such an expert with the big wide outdoors—"

"But the blood on the stock of his gun?"

"If he was attacked by a gator he would have gotten a shot off," Hunter said. "We need to find out if he did. Anyway, if he wasn't killed by a predator his death must be connected to one of his deployments overseas."

"Yep, I agree with you. He pissed someone off and they wanted rid of him."

"Which implies he was into something he shouldn't have been. So we need to find out where he was deployed. We'll get Raoul to do some digging into his archives for us."

Lewis chuckled. "You mean the military's archives."

"Whatever." Hunter paused to savor his wine. The rich ruby liquid trickled down his throat, taking the edge off his discontent. "What was her apartment really like?"

"Not as bad as I figured it would be. Nothing else was taken but for her computer and probably some papers. Cupboards were pulled open but it wasn't trashed. I put everything back and tidied up so it won't be too much of a shock for her when she moves back in."

"That was thoughtful."

Lewis shrugged. "You know me. It was just that lipstick thing on the bathroom mirror that was freaky, but I cleaned it off, too. She had some bits of jewelry in a box and they weren't taken."

"Definitely not the military then. They don't leave messages in lipstick."

"Nah, they prefer blood."

"We need to get some clues on who we're dealing with so we know where to start looking. I'll call Raoul after dinner and set him to work. Right now, I need to finish off in the kitchen."

"I'll open another bottle," Lewis said.

Anais joined them just as Hunter was serving up the food. Both men turned to look at her and whistled in unison. It was the first time Hunter had seen her with her hair down. The wait had been worth it. It cascaded around her shoulders in a riot of curls, and he itched to run his fingers through its thickness. She wore no makeup, but then she didn't need to, and had put on a light, floaty sundress—no bra. She looked good enough to lick. All over.

She blushed beneath their admiring glances, and reached for the salad bowl still on the kitchen counter.

"Here, let me help."

"We've got it covered," Lewis replied. "Come and sit down, darlin', and we'll get you some more wine."

Hunter sensed Anais relaxing as the wine did its work on her nerves, and his food warmed her insides. He and Lewis entertained her with chat that had nothing to do with her problems, and she appeared to appreciate taking a break from them. Hunter tried not to imagine how much strain she'd been living under these past two years, and especially recently since she had decided to look into her husband's death and hit so many brick walls. If he let his sympathy take over, he would be worse than useless to her.

"You guys are such good housekeepers," she said at one point. "I'm surprised you don't have kids. You'd make great dads."

Hunter and Lewis shared a glance. "Neither of us is fixated on procreation," Hunter said. "Don't get me wrong," he added with a sexy smile, "we like the theory part. We're definitely up for all the work that goes into making kids, it's the responsibility that goes with parenthood that puts us off."

"Oh, but it doesn't have to be scary. It's supposed to be the most fulfilling job in the world," she replied with a wistful sigh.

"Kids don't come with an instruction manual though, do they, darlin'?" Lewis asked.

"Sorry," Anais said, grinning at them both. "I've obviously touched a nerve. Besides, it's none of my business."

"It's just something we feel kinda strongly about," Hunter said, topping off her glass.

They finished their meal talking about other stuff. With the dishes stacked in the dishwasher, Hunter showed Anais into the airy room he and Lewis used as a study.

"Here you go," he said, pulling out a chair at one of the desks. "Feel free to call this laptop your own. I suggest you load your stuff onto it, while I call Raoul and bring him up to speed with your problems. You okay with that?"

"Yes, don't worry about me. I don't need entertaining."

It was on the tip of his tongue to ask what she did need, but Hunter manfully restrained himself. He left her to it and made his calls. She was at the laptop for over an hour and when she emerged from the study, she was stifling a yawn.

"That's it," Hunter said, standing. "You need to get some rest. You said earlier you haven't been sleeping well. Go hit the sack."

"You're right, perhaps I will call it a night. In the morning I'll show you all the records I have of Gary's stuff. It's on your laptop now."

"That would be great."

Lewis made do with waving and blowing her a kiss. Hunter knew what he would infinitely prefer to do, because he felt the exact same way.

"Sleep well, darlin'," he said.

* * * *

Sleep well. That was easy for them to say. She *was* tired, weary to the bone, and the thought of sleeping a full eight hours, secure in the knowledge that no one could get to her, was almost as intoxicating as the excess wine she had drunk. But Anais knew almost as soon as her head hit the pillow that it wasn't going to happen. Her mind simply refused to shut down. She was used to working solo and found it hard to cede control, sit back and let others do the worrying for her.

Why were bad guys with access to tracking devices so keen for her to stop looking into her husband's death, she wondered. *What did you get yourself into, Gary?* Whatever it was, the people trying to warn her off seemed to think she knew. Did she? Had she discovered something significant without realizing it?

Hunter and Lewis seemed confident they could get to the bottom of things, but could they? It wasn't the military who had stolen her computer and threatened her. The guys hadn't said as much, but she wasn't completely stupid and had worked that much out for herself. She was annoyed with them for holding out on her, but at the same time enjoyed feeling cosseted and protected. How girly was that? In her own defense, it had been a while since anyone gave a shit about her, including Gary, she thought with a jolt. Especially Gary. All the time he had been posted overseas she hadn't felt lonely because he was still the old Gary she had fallen for. But something had changed about the same time as his career took a nosedive. Once he was with her all the time, she felt more lonely than when they were separated.

Anais admitted to herself then something she hadn't been ready to acknowledge before now. She had fallen out of love with Gary before he died. There, she'd said it, if only inside her head. It was a liberating feeling, too. Gary had given her the cold shoulder, cut her out of his life, and what they had once shared was beyond redemption. Was that why she had tried to find out what happened to him? To assuage her guilt?

Possibly.

Gary's loss wasn't the only reason why she was unable to sleep. Hunter and Lewis occupied way more of her thoughts than they should. She was curious about them and, if she was honest, totally turned on by the way they both looked at her as though they were mentally undressing her. More than one man had hit on her over the years, assuming she was a lonely soldier's wife in need of a little fun. None of them had come close to tempting her. And yet now she was fantasizing about not one, but two disturbingly poised males. She told herself she was being ridiculous, but her body was having none of it. They had woken her up in all respects, but were now presumably sleeping down the hall from her, oblivious to her frustration.

It was all very well for them, she thought moodily. Hunter had told her they didn't have women in their lives. Maybe not permanent fixtures, she thought mutinously, but she was willing to be bet they were active players. Guys who looked as good as they did were hardly likely to lead celibate lives, but had made it obvious they never mixed business with pleasure. And they looked upon her as a business assignment.

Damn!

She had finally gotten to the stage where she might want to broaden her sexual horizons and the guy—make that guys—she'd be willing to do it with were off limits.

Anais tried to tear her thoughts away from her hosts by returning them to Gary. Perhaps there was something she had overlooked on her computer that had gotten her noticed by the guys threatening her.

Giving up on sleep, she threw back the covers and padded quietly downstairs, wearing just the oversized T-shirt she slept in. She didn't want to wake the guys, but she did want to take a look at everything she had so far compiled with a fresh eye. If that failed, she'd simply get on with some editing until she was ready to sleep.

In the end, she did neither of those things. Instead she scrolled through all the photographs she had downloaded from her memory stick, a visual reminder of her life with Gary going back to their college days. Tears streamed down her face without her being aware of them. Their relationship had gone horribly wrong, but so slowly she had barely noticed the changes until they were no longer communicating and it was too late to fix whatever had broken. She hadn't expected the hearts and roses stage to continue, but had never expected to lose Gary either, which she now accepted is what had happened. *What were you into, Gary? Why didn't you feel you could share your problems with me?*

She became aware of a presence and looked up to see Hunter standing in the open doorway. She gasped at the sight of his bare chest. His bare everything. The boxers he wore were barely adequate to cover his genitalia. The sight of such a fine specimen of the masculine form took her breath away, and she didn't seem able to look away from him.

"I heard a noise," he said softly. "Are you okay?" She nodded, her throat too clogged for her to be able to speak. "Hey, you're crying? What is it?"

He was beside her then, wiping the tears from her face with such a gentle touch that she was lost to all reason. All her pent up emotions, the feelings she had been holding in check for so long, bubbled to the surface and her trickle of tears turned into a flood. She wasn't sure quite how it happened, but the next thing she knew, Hunter was sitting in a comfortable love seat in the corner of his office, and she was on his lap, her arms twined around his neck.

Chapter Five

This so shouldn't be happening, even though Hunter had known it would the moment he saw she was crying. His self-restraint could definitely use some work but, in his own defense, he'd always been a sucker for a woman's tears. Shit, she wasn't wearing a goddamned thing beneath that T-shirt. Not even panties. He knew it the moment he lifted her from her chair and into his lap, but he didn't let it stop him. He wasn't wearing a whole lot of anything himself. Jeez! He was in deep trouble, but knowing it and resisting his deep fascination for their highly addictive client were too very different matters.

Anais's tears had dried up and she looked at him through eyes that smoldered with something other than distress. Eyes that suddenly seemed way too large for her fragile face. Eyes that were asking an age-old question, although he was unsure if she realized it.

"I'd best take you back to your room," he said, his voice rough, ragged.

"I won't be able to sleep."

"You might surprise yourself."

"I want to stay with you." She looked as taken aback as he felt when she said the words, almost as though she didn't intend for them to be said aloud. "Don't send me away."

"Honey, what you're asking me. It's not a good idea."

She maintained steady eye contact with him, her highly-kissable lips way too close to his, a slight frown marring her brow. "You don't want me?"

"Now you know better than that." Hunter expelled a throaty chuckle. "I think the evidence speaks for itself."

She sent him a smug smile. "Well then."

"Anais, you're in a highly emotional state right now. You don't really know what you want. I don't want to take advantage of your vulnerability."

"This is too embarrassing for words." She shook her head, sending a cascade of hair tumbling over her face. Helpless, Hunter reached up a hand and tucked it back behind her ear. "I'm throwing myself at you, and you don't want to know."

Shit, now he had upset her. He ran a hand down the length of her back, bringing it to rest not on her backside, which was his stopping point of choice, but innocently on the small of her back. "In case you still haven't gotten the message, I want you so much it's frigging painful, especially when you don't sit still."

She stifled a giggle. "Then what's stopping you?"

"We've been called in to sort out your problems, not add to them."

How had her lips gotten even closer to his? He was sure he hadn't moved his head, but somehow the distance between their mouths was now almost nonexistent. Her sweet breath peppered his face as the little vixen moistened her lower lip with the tip of her tongue and sent him a sultry smile. Shit! Hunter growled, thrust his hands into her hair and tugged her head down until that small gap was no longer there at all. He kissed her hard, with authority, like a man with a point to prove, but whether he was proving something to himself or to her was less obvious. His tongue plundered her mouth, savoring its sweetness, and the kiss became unashamedly carnal.

His hands drifted beneath her T-shirt and ran up her torso until one of them covered a small, firm breast. His fingers explored, laying claim, wanting her like he hadn't wanted a woman since forever. She moaned past their fused lips as he plucked at her solidified nipple, pinching it between his fingers and tugging it away from her body.

"Are you sure you want this, babe?" he asked.

"I was never more sure of anything," she replied, her lips shiny and wet as the words slipped past them.

"Then there's something you need to know first."

She tangled her fingers in his hair and sent him a provocative smile. "What?"

"Well, Lewis and I are a package deal."

Her eyes flew open. "A what?"

"We're sexual Doms. Do you know what that is?"

"I've edited more than my fair share of erotic literature, so I know what you like to do, but I've never tried it."

"You don't seem fazed by the idea."

She blinked back her surprise. "Are you saying the two of you like to share a woman?"

"Yeah, pretty much."

"Good."

"You're okay with that?" It was Hunter's turn to express surprise. "I thought you'd run a mile when I told you the truth."

"Oh no, you don't get rid of me that easily. I felt drawn to you both from the word go. I tried to tell myself it was just because you'd helped me out when I was scared, but I knew there was more to it than that." She traced the line of his lips with her forefinger. "It explains a lot about the way you guys live here together."

"I take it you've never been dominated before. Gary wasn't into that, or anyone since."

"Gary wasn't what you'd call a Dom, I don't think so anyway. In fact I'm sure of it." She looked directly at him, happy to discuss sex with him, but not to go into detail about her personal life with Gary. He might be dead, but it still seemed disloyal somehow. "And there's never been anyone else. I already told you that."

Now she had really surprised him. "I know you were faithful when Gary was alive, but surely since then, there must have been guys."

"Oh, a few have tried, but I wasn't ready."

"I understand you must be beyond frustrated—"

"Well, I have a good collection of vibrators, but it's not the same."

"That I'd pay good money to see." He grinned at her. "You with a huge vibrator inside your pussy." Shit, now why had he said that? It would only encourage her, but perhaps that was subconsciously what he was trying to do. "But seriously, in spite of what you think, you're not ready to play with us. Not with two of us at once, which is how we operate. Not only that, but we...well, we like it hard and rough. We're into bondage and all sorts of other kinky stuff that I'm betting you've never tried."

"Then it's about time I did, and I just happen to have found two pretty experienced teachers."

He resisted the urge to reclaim her nipple. "It wouldn't be fair."

"I need this, Hunter. I need you both, no strings attached." She sent him a beseeching smile and locked her hands firmly at the back of his neck. "Please!"

There was no way in this world he could resist such a direct request. Longing flowed between them like crystal-clear water, sapping at Hunter's dwindling resistance. She wanted this, so did he, and there was no reason in the world why they shouldn't get it on.

There's every reason.

"Oh, honey, you don't know what you're asking for."

"I want to feel alive again. I've had enough of marking time, waiting for something to happen. I realize now that's what I've been doing." She released her death grip on his neck and buried her fingers in his hair instead. "I've been waiting for you and Lewis to wake me up. It seems right and natural that you guys should be the ones. Don't tell me you don't feel it, too."

"Okay, sweetness, if you're absolutely sure. But you'll have to make do with me for now. Lewis will just have to wait his turn. We'll get you used to things real slow." He felt vindicated in dropping a hand to her backside this time, lifting her briefly so he could caress her pussy from beneath. Honey trickled from her cunt, confirming for Hunter that she really did want to play.

"You will have to do whatever we ask of you without question. That's part of the fun."

"And I have to call you Master or Sir," she said with a sultry giggle.

He tweaked her nose. "You *have* done your reading."

"Yes, Sir, I have."

"We'll teach you to embrace pain, and to enjoy it, darlin', if you'll let us." He pushed her hair aside and trailed kisses down the length of her neck. When she reacted by squirming, he introduced his teeth. "Do you like that?"

"Hmm, yes, Sir."

"Then let's see if you enjoy having that cute butt spanked." He tipped her off his knee. "Stand up and take your T-shirt off for me. I want to look at you."

She did as he asked, standing a few feet in front of him, backlit by the Anglepoise lamp on the desk behind her. Hunter inhaled sharply when her delectable body was revealed to him, confirming what he already knew about her. Her tits were firm and pert, the nipples puckered, the areolas a deep raspberry pink crying out to be devoured by his hungry mouth. Her belly was flat, her thighs trim, her legs endless. Better yet, her pussy was shaved as opposed to waxed—just the way a woman's cunt should be. She was so goddamned perfect, Hunter felt all his Christmases had come together. He felt unworthy, and uncharacteristically unsure of himself.

She met his gaze, her face flushed—with embarrassment or excitement Hunter couldn't have said. No, it was definitely excitement. The hungry sparkle in her eyes gave her away. Hunter nodded slowly, making his approval apparent to her.

"You're really up for this, ain't you, sugar?"

"Hmm."

He reached forward and tapped her thigh. Hard. "Did you just say something?"

"I said yes, Sir," she replied, biting her lower lip in a manner that did strange things to Hunter's psyche.

"Come kneel on this rug, rest your head and arms on the seat and stick your butt in the air," he said. "You've been a bad girl and need to be chastised."

"Yes, Sir."

Hunter watched her as she eagerly got herself into position, wondering what the fuck he thought he was doing. It wouldn't kill him to have vanilla sex for once, and work up to the rest, instead of introducing a woman who had only ever known one man straight into his lifestyle. But something stronger than his own will drove him on, and he managed to convince himself this was what she had been saving herself for. She certainly didn't seem to have any doubts.

Decided, Hunter threw off his shorts and knelt behind her, one hand possessively spanning the small globes of her ass.

"Normally I would have your hands tied before I did this to you," he said, leaning down and gently nipping at one buttock. "But I figure you need to get used to our ways gradually. Now then, honey, I'm going to spank some obedience into you, then I'm gonna fuck you senseless. You good with that?"

"Yes, Master, it's what I want you to do."

He brought his hand down hard, without warning her to expect it. She cried out and jerked her head up.

"Shush, keep quiet and hold your position." He leaned forward to lick the area he had just spanked. "Just breathe real deep and wait for the slight pain to become pleasurable." He grabbed his rigid cock and ran it down the crack in her butt, letting her get a good feel for it. "Just imagine how you'll feel with this filling your tight cunt, darlin'."

She panted. "Yes, Sir, I already am."

He spanked her a second time, feeling beneath her at the same time and sliding a couple of fingers into her slick pussy. This time she took it without flinching.

"That's a good girl. You're a real quick study. I'm very pleased with you. You okay?"

"Yes, Sir. It hurts, but in a good way."

Hunter chuckled. "That's the idea. Every time you sit down tomorrow you'll be a little bit uncomfortable and it will remind you of what we're about to do."

Hunter brought his hand down three more times in quick succession, then told her to stand up. She did so and her eyes widened when she caught sight of Hunter naked, his cock jutting aggressively, pulsating, ready for action.

"Yes, baby, if you're a real good girl I'll fill your sweet cunt with this guy in a short time. But first, those tits of yours need some attention. Lay down on the love seat."

Hunter followed her down, laying on his side as his hands went to work, caressing and molding her lovely breasts, tweaking at the nipples, playing with her, lighting her fires. Her hands came to rest on the back of his neck, which told him it was time to tie her up. She had yet to learn patience, obedience and passivity when aroused. Without explaining himself, he removed her hands and abruptly got up. He dashed naked across the living room, into the guys' private play room off the back of the garage. He grabbed handcuffs and a condom packet and returned to Anais, who hadn't moved a muscle.

"Arms above your head," he said curtly.

He cuffed her wrists as soon as she complied. "Leave them right where they are," he said, adding a blindfold for good measure. "You sure do look pretty that way, and just about as helpless as it's possible to get. This is all about trust, you see. You need to trust me to give you pleasure, and the blindfold and lack of touch will enhance your other senses, like taste." He leaned over her and held the tip of his cock to her lips. "See what that tastes like, sweetheart."

"Hmm, hot," she mumbled as her mouth closed around him.

Hunter chuckled and sighed simultaneously as he pulled out of her mouth again. She had got him so riled up that his usual method of control was slipping. If he let her carry on for long, this would all be over in a flash. He returned his attention to her tits, biting at the solid nipples, and was rewarded by a series of increasingly desperate moans from his sub-in-training.

"I get the impression you like that, sugar."

"Yes, Master, I like it a lot."

"Hmm, next time we'll put some clamps on those cute tits of yours, then you'll really feel something special."

Hunter knelt on the rug beside the love seat, threw Anais's legs over his shoulders and gave his full attention to her pussy. She was leaking juices big time now, and started moaning all over again before he had even touched her. She was so damned responsive, so made for this type of loving. He had never indoctrinated a sub from scratch before. All the women he and Lewis played with were already into the life. Introducing someone as greedy for knowledge at Anais was both a privilege and a tad scary. In his enthusiasm, Hunter might go too far. Shit, he hadn't even discussed safe words with her. What sort of responsible Dom did that make him?

"If I do anything you don't like, darlin', you can tell me to stop any time. You need a safe word. What word can you easily remember if needs be?"

"Split infinitive," she replied.

Hunter chuckled. "Ever the editor. Okay, split infinitive it is."

Hunter lapped at the juices trickling down her inner thighs, and then applied his tongue to her clit. She cried out and thrust her pussy deeper into his mouth. Shit, she was killing him!

"Keep still!" He tapped her raised butt hard.

"Sorry, Master."

"If you move without permission, I'll stop what I'm doing. Are we clear?"

"That is so mean."

"That's the way this game is played. I'm in charge and you only get to feel what I allow you to."

* * * *

This was the sweetest agony Anais had ever known. It was also strangely familiar, even though she'd never done anything remotely like it before. Gary had always been a lights off, missionary position sort of guy. Not that he hadn't given her pleasure, but she understood now that the depths of her passions had barely been plumbed. She had always felt vaguely dissatisfied, but had nothing to compare Gary's lovemaking to and so didn't understand why. Now she did. Before the act had even taken place her body was on fire in a way she'd never known before. It felt disloyal to compare what she was feeling now to her years of marriage to Gary, but it was an impossible comparison not to make. Hunter's tongue, his lips, his teeth knew exactly where to torment her to give her maximum pleasure without actually letting her climax. She so badly needed to come, and this torture was...well, torturous. It was exquisite, it was fun, it was liberating.

What had she been missing all these years? No, she hadn't been missing out. She'd been waiting for the right person—the right people—to come wake her up. Had she really agreed to go with them both? Would they want her both at once? Would they want anal sex? Well, of course they would! The answer was *yes* to all those questions, and Anais briefly panicked. But only very briefly. Hunter's marauding tongue recalled her to the here and now. The muscles in her belly clenched against the pleasure he was stirring deep within her core. She felt molten heat flood her system, and rushing, soaring excitement addle her brain.

Anais still had trouble believing what she'd seen before Hunter blindfolded her. The size of his cock was the answer to every girl's most erotic fantasy and, for now at least, it was all hers. It was about to fill her, stretch her, and give her relief from the endless pressure she'd been living with for so long without really being aware of it.

Bring it on!

As though sensing her impatience, Hunter abruptly abandoned his pussy feast. She heard him stand up, the sound of a foil packet being ripped open greeted her, and then he was with her again, his body a hot prison above hers. She expected him to say something, to warn her what to expect. Instead, he threw her legs over his shoulders again, and told her to lift her butt. She did so and felt cushions being pushed beneath it. Then the tip of his latex-covered cock dipped into her pussy and he thrust powerfully into her, grunting from the effort it took him. This position meant he went deep, deeper than she would have imagined possible, but Anais wasn't complaining. She groaned as pleasure beyond her wildest imagination assailed her from all sides. Hunter was splitting her open with his thick, throbbing cock, filling her to capacity, stretching the sensitized walls of her cunt to the absolute limit.

It was the most intense sensation, and Anais greedily tightened the muscles in her pussy around his length. She didn't want him to withdraw, even though she knew he was only doing so in order to pummel right back into her again, a little more harshly with each sortie. His heavy balls crashed against her buttocks, and he occasionally administered a harsh slap to her backside as he took her closer to the abyss.

With her cuffed wrists above her head, her eyes covered with a blindfold, Anais soon discovered Hunter had been honest with her. Not being able to see or touch really did heighten her awareness as she felt herself rapidly climbing higher with every powerful gyration of Hunter's hips.

"That's it, babe, now you've got it all. You liking that?"

"Yes, Sir. God, yes! I feel violated, in a good way. Does that make sense?"

"I don't aim to demean you, darlin', but I did warn you I like it hard and rough."

She grinned. "So do I, it seems."

"I got that part."

She could hear the smile in his voice, and the strain. He wasn't nearly as in control as he would have her think. She would have bruises tomorrow, but she didn't give a damn. Right now she was living, really living, and that was all that mattered to her. She felt a kernel of sensation uncoil inside her, unfamiliar and primitive, even though she recognized it as her climax building. She'd had countless orgasms before, both with Gary and at her own hand, but they had been nothing to the way she felt now. The intoxicating friction of his cock against the walls of her cunt was in danger of short-circuiting her brain, and she moaned, thrashing her head from side to side as she fought to hold off the inevitable. He hadn't given her permission to come, and she didn't want it to be over with yet.

But the feelings were too strong, too urgent, and she couldn't hold them off.

"Hunter, I—"

"I know."

He thrust into her deeper and harder than before, which was saying something. She tightened and clenched around him, and her world imploded. She cried out, not caring who heard her as a deeply disturbing thrill rocked her entire body, sending it into a series of violent spasms. She felt perspiration dripping from her brow, and peppering the rest of her body. She didn't care about that either.

When she came back to earth, Hunter was still rock hard inside her, and she sensed they were no longer alone. Her cries had obviously disturbed Lewis.

"Have we had a change of rules you didn't tell me about?" she heard Lewis ask.

"Sorry, buddy," Hunter replied. "The lady couldn't sleep, and well—"

"Don't mind me," Lewis chuckled. "Finish what you started. Something tells me our house guest won't be satisfied with just one."

One what? Orgasm? Man? He must mean he wanted her, too. Anais had never had more than one orgasm at a time, so that must be it. Except…except Hunter was moving inside of her again, and she felt fingers pinching her nipples. They couldn't be Hunter's because he was using one hand to slap her butt and the other to hold her wrists down. Oh my, someone was biting at a nipple. She moaned. It had to be Lewis. His fingers dug harshly into the fleshy parts of her tits, while his teeth put steadily increasing pressure on her nipple. Hunter was working her cunt harder than ever. She could hear his labored breathing, and sensed he was close.

Damn it, so was she. This was beyond sensual.

"Guys, please, I—"

"Told you so," said a smug-sounding Lewis.

"Let it go, babe," Hunter said. "Let's get there together."

"You like having Hunter's cock inside you, darlin'? You just wait until you have mine. The two of us will take you places you never knew existed. Trust me on this."

The sexy words, the return of Lewis's teeth to her nipple, the feel of Hunter's cock fucking her senseless—the combination was lethal and once again her world fragmented. This time Hunter followed her over the edge, paddling her ass hard as she sensed an endless flow of hot sperm shooting into the condom.

"Hey, welcome back," Hunter said a short time later as she lay panting and sweaty between two hot bodies. The blindfold and handcuffs were removed and two handsome, smiling faces came into focus.

"Next time you plan a party, make sure you invite me along," Lewis said, pouting.

"It was spontaneous." Anais grinned, thinking the entire world should be grinning right along with her. "I had to talk Hunter into it. He didn't want to."

Lewis laughed. "I could see how much he didn't want to."

"I changed his mind for him."

"You okay, darlin'?" Hunter asked. "I was kinda harsh with you there."

"You warned me you would be and I loved it." She smiled at them both. "When can we do it again? I have lost time to make up for."

Lewis grimaced and placed a hand over his cock, which was covered by a pair of very small briefs. "I'm in pain here, but I also happen to know you're new to this. We'll get you cleaned up and tuck you up in bed. I'll take a rain check."

"Aw."

Both men chuckled. "I've awoken a beast," Hunter said.

"Looks that way," Lewis agreed. "Seems to me she was always supposed to be one of us. I should have recognized the signs."

In spite of her best efforts, she couldn't persuade either man to make love to her again. They wiped her clean, but she was too lazy to take a shower. An hour ago she couldn't sleep to save her life. Now she had discovered the ultimate cure for insomnia. Her last thought before falling into a blissful sleep was to wonder if she could patent the remedy. She would be set up for life if she could.

Chapter Six

Hunter and Lewis were both up early. Hunter set the coffee going, knowing Lewis would cut to the chase. He didn't disappoint.

"So, what brought about the change of heart?" he asked. "Not that I'm complaining or anything, but you were adamant we keep things all business with Anais."

"What can I say?" Hunter flashed a sheepish smile. "She caught me at a weak moment."

Lewis rolled his eyes. "Of course she did."

"I heard her moving around so I got up to see if there was a problem. She was crying, and…well I had to—"

Lewis grinned. "Yeah, I get the picture."

"Actually you don't. I told her it wasn't a good idea, and I meant it, but she insisted." Hunter flashed a smug smile. "And get this, she's only been with one man her entire life."

Lewis's brows snapped together. "You're kidding me? She hasn't been with anyone since her husband died."

"Nope." Hunter shrugged. "Well, not until last night."

"No wonder she couldn't resist your rather obvious charm." Hunter flipped Lewis the finger. "And now she wants to take up with us both? Please tell me I didn't manfully resist her last night only for her to have a change of heart this morning."

"So she said last night and…well, you saw for yourself how abandoned she was. I gotta say, she's a natural, but in the cold light of day I wonder if our lifestyle will be too much for her."

"You ask me, I think we'll have a tough time stopping her from experimenting. It's like she's just realized what she's been missing out on and wants to make up for lost time."

Hunter smirked as he poured coffee for them both. "Or you just wanna get laid."

"Yeah well, there's that, too."

"Well, I guess we can still be professional *and* have some fun. We kinda have an added incentive to get her out of this mess now."

"Too right we do."

"I'll hold breakfast until Anais comes down. She was pretty beat, poor baby. Best to let her sleep. I don't think she's been sleeping too well lately."

"I can think of a whole load of ways to help her sleep."

Hunter shot him a look. "We need to take things slow."

"Didn't see you going too slow last night."

"That was different."

"So what are you saying? You don't think she'll want me to wake her up with a cup of tea and a big…err, smile?"

Hunter chuckled. "I'm sure she would appreciate the size of your smile. But not right now. We need to take a look at some stuff, get a handle on how we're gonna fight back against the goons trying to frighten our girl."

"Our girl. I like the sound of that."

"Okay," Hunter said as Lewis followed him into their study. "I called Raoul last night asking him to see what he could find on the investigation into Gary's disappearance. You know how quickly he can hack into stuff. There might be news."

They were unsurprised to find an e-mail from Raoul, with attachments.

"It's the military file into Gary's disappearance," Lewis said, punching the air. "Way to go, Raoul."

Hunter didn't answer. He was into Raoul's e-mail, and Lewis read it over his shoulder.

"I knew it," Lewis said. "There *is* more to this than a straightforward accident."

"Looks that way," Hunter agreed. "Raoul says we won't find much in the attached file, and that the main investigation is now eyes-only."

That was a euphemism for the investigation becoming top secret and the details being kept in paper form only. Paradoxically, a number of organizations paranoid about security had reverted to keeping just one or two copies of sensitive documents in paper form only. Given that averagely intelligent computer-savvy teens had repeatedly proven they could hack into just about any online facility from the privacy of their own bedrooms, Hunter could understand the retrograde step. Still, it made him wonder what Sergeant Harrison had gotten himself into to cause the top brass to get its collective panties in a wad.

"Curious," he said to Lewis.

"Something tells me our Gary wasn't as clean cut as his wife would have us believe."

"Evidently not."

"Raoul hasn't been able to find out what foreign attachments Gary was a part of." Lewis grinned. "I bet that pissed him off."

"Yeah, and I bet it won't take him much longer to find out. But in the meantime." Hunter clicked to open the attachment. "Let's see what the official record has to say about his disappearance."

Lewis pulled up a chair and the two guys studied the report together, starting with pictures of where Harrison's rifle had been found. There were close-ups of the stock, covered in blood, and longer-range shots of the gun in situ. Hunter zoomed in on the shots, examining them minutely. He then read the report that led to the find.

"Hmm, this position is a seldom-used trail that was soft underfoot, not close to any water." He paused. "Notice anything about the terrain, buddy?"

"Yeah," Lewis replied without hesitation. "No footprints other than one set leading to the rifle, which are presumably Gary's, no disturbed foliage or signs of a struggle."

"Right." Hunter ran one hand through his hair. "We know gators don't only stick to the swamp, so we can't rule out the possibility of him being attacked by one, but if he was—"

"If he was, there would be all sorts of signs."

"Right, and that would have set alarm bells ringing for the investigators. It was the first thing we noticed, and they would have done, too."

"You think the scene was staged? Gary faked his own death?"

"I'm trying to keep an open mind, but my initial thoughts are that it looks that way. He was too good with the outdoors to be caught by a rogue gator, or anything else living in the 'Glades. Something is definitely off about this."

"We already knew that," Lewis pointed out. "It's not the military trying to scare the shit out of Anais."

The guys flipped through the pictures of the scene. Apart from Gary's rifle, all that was found was a strip of material from his fatigues, or what was assumed to be his fatigues. The investigators thought it must be his because it was too fresh and clean to have been there for long. The written report didn't draw any conclusions, but listed the people who had been spoken to after the disappearance.

"Harrison left the other three instructors to do a spot check on some of the trainees," Hunter read, noting down the names of Gary's fellow trainers. "He always insisted on going alone, even though it was against regulations and they were supposed to go in pairs."

"Sounds as though he was a lone wolf."

"Yeah. When he didn't return, the others searched the area where he said he would be, but there was no sign of him. His gun was eventually found in a sector where no trainees were supposed to be, so Gary had no reason to go there."

"No legitimate reason, anyway."

"Right," Hunter agreed. "And that's where the report, such as it is, goes all secret."

Hunter returned his attention to Raoul's e-mail. Ever efficient, he'd found the names of the other three instructors on the course.

"One has been returned to active duties and is currently deployed overseas," he said, "so we can't talk to him. Mike Pearson is still in the service, but lives off base, and we have an address and phone number for him. Tony Regan got invalided out last year but still lives locally. Raoul has come through with his details, too."

"Right," Lewis said. "Looks like we need to start by talking to them. They were probably in deep shit for letting Harrison go off on his own so were busy covering their backs when spoken to officially. They might have more to say to us."

"Hey."

They both turned to see Anais standing in the doorway, clearly fresh from the shower, damp hair tumbling down her back. She wore tight-fitting jeans and a sleeveless top, and looked a little embarrassed, as though unsure of her reception.

"Hey yourself." Hunter sent her a killer smile. "You okay?"

"Err, yes."

Lewis stood up and gave her a kiss. "Did you sleep well?"

"Actually, yes." She blushed. "Better than I have for ages."

"That's what mind-blowing sex does to a body," Hunter said, keen to get the subject out in the open. If she had regrets, now was the time to say so. Neither man would be happy if she tried to dodge the issue.

"So it would seem." She hugged her torso and briefly met Hunter's eye. He exhaled, glad to realize she was afflicted with nothing more permanent than embarrassment. It would, of course make his life far less complicated if she'd had a change of heart, but Hunter desperately didn't want her to do the sensible thing. There was just something about Anais, and he was already in too deep to pull back. She wandered farther into the room and peered over Hunter's shoulder. "What are you doing?"

"Looking at the official report into Gary's disappearance, but there isn't much of it." Hunter explained about the investigation becoming top secret. Anais appeared stunned by the news.

"Why?" she asked. "Gary wasn't that important."

Hunter wasn't ready to share his theories with her. "That's what we need to find out. Do you know either of these guys, Mike Pearson and Tony Regan? They were also instructors on that survival course."

"I think I met them a few times at the base on social occasions, but I don't really know them."

"Well, I shall pay them a call today, see what they can tell me."

"I'll come with you."

"No, babe, better if I go alone. You stay here and keep Lewis company."

"But why?"

"You don't wanna keep me company?" Lewis affected a hurt expression. "Is it something I said?"

"No, silly. But everyone was real nice to me after Gary disappeared and…well, they'll probably talk openly to me."

Not if Gary wasn't the upstanding guy she supposed him to be, Hunter thought. "Leave it to me."

Hunter closed the computer down and stood up. "Come on, we could all use some breakfast."

Hunter cooked for them all, amused to see that Anais, who had only picked at her food the previous evening, had a voracious appetite this morning. Another benefit of hot sex, he thought.

He left Lewis and Anais to clear up while he went back to the study and called the numbers for both of Gary's colleagues. He caught a break in that they were both home, and willing to talk to him.

"Okay guys, I'm out of here." He picked up the keys to their truck from the hall stand and leaned down to kiss the top of Anais's head. "Play nice without me."

* * * *

"Is he always so decisive?" Anais asked, staring after Hunter.

Lewis grinned as he drained his coffee. "Yeah, pretty much, but we love him anyway."

Anais looked as though she didn't know what to do with herself. Lewis had a few ideas about how to distract her. He knew that was partly why Hunter had left them alone, but in spite of the raging lust that gripped him whenever he was anywhere near her, he wouldn't push her into anything. It was way too soon, and she was still pretty fragile.

"Wanna catch a few rays outside on the deck?" he asked.

"No thanks."

"Oh, okay, then what would you like to do?"

She sent him a dazzling smile. "I think you know."

Lewis shook his head. "There's no pressure, darlin'."

"Oh yes there is. You guys started this thing. I need to know what happens next." Her sultry expression was full of newfound awareness. "My education is sadly lacking."

"We can't have that now, can we?" Lewis offered her a wicked smile. "But I'm worried you might be sore. I'm betting Hunter paddled your sweet ass last night. It's what he does."

"Yes, he did." Her smile widened but gave way to a wince when she wiggled about in her chair. "It's a little tender, but in a good way. It reminds me of what I've been missing out on all these years."

"Well, if you're okay, I guess I could be persuaded."

She tossed her head. "Only if it's not too much trouble. I mean, we could talk, and stuff."

"For you, darlin', I don't mind how much trouble I get into." His cock was already standing up and taking avid interest in the proceedings. He hoped she didn't notice. The last thing he wanted was for her to think he was forcing himself on her, even if his intentions had been far from innocent ever since Hunter deliberately left them alone. He joined her on the settee, and ran his arm along the back of it, twisting a lock of her hair around his finger. "What would you like to talk about?"

She grinned. "How long have you got?"

"All the time in the world." He dropped a light kiss on her lips. "Just so that you know, there's nowhere else I'd rather be."

"You don't have to sweet talk me."

"Hey, you need to learn to take a compliment."

"Sorry, I guess I'm still a bit new to all this."

"I don't want you to feel uncomfortable, or obligated."

She wagged a finger at him. "Are you trying to wiggle out of *your* obligations?"

He caught her finger and sucked it into his mouth. "Not a chance."

"Tell me about you and Hunter," she said, blushing again. "You guys seem kind of tight. Did you meet in the military?"

"Yeah. I had an easy time of it as a kid. Came from a middle class family, with a full set of parents and siblings. No drama, no abuse. My only problem was I got picked on a lot because I was puny."

She glanced at his torso and flexed a brow. "I find that hard to believe."

"Oh, believe it. I have the military to thank for muscling me up."

She laughed. "Most people content themselves with joining a gym if they want to get in shape."

"Baby, I'm not most people. I got out of college with a degree in mechanical engineering, but with no clear idea of what I wanted to do next. I knew Hunter from high school. He skipped college and went straight into the army because he had a crap family life and wanted something to take him away from being a fulltime parent to his brothers and sister."

"Oh, that does sound tough. How did he find himself in that situation?"

"You'll have to ask Hunter if you want to know more. Even I don't know it all, but I can tell you it wasn't all white picket fences and apple pie for him. Far from it. He was a bit of a lost cause when I knew him, and I couldn't believe the difference when we met again."

"The army made a man out of him," Anais suggested, grinning.

"Yeah, it got me thinking along the same lines and the rest, as they say, is history."

She drained her coffee mug and placed it aside. "I'm not a great fan of the military. Wives don't always have a good time of it, but I do know most of the guys feel a great sense of camaraderie."

"When you have one another's backs in life and death situations there has to be trust." Lewis sensed Anais's eyes lingering on his torso, and lower.

"You have my trust." She placed a hand on his bicep. "But I believe we have unfinished business."

"Are you sure?" He met her gaze, caressing her with his eyes. "I don't want to put pressure on you."

She bit her lip, as though trying to hold in a giggle. "I don't believe you."

"Well, I do want to play with you, very much, as it happens. Why should Hunter have all the fun? But you have to want it, too."

"I do." She drilled him with an intent look. "What Hunter did to me was awesome, and I want more of the same. I really want to play. Sir."

"Okay, darlin', let's take this upstairs." He took her hand and helped her up. "We're gonna take a bath together, and if you're a real naughty girl, I'll scrub your back for you."

"Only my back?"

Lewis growled, kicked open the door to her room, and pulled her straight into his arms. Her lovely tits crashed against his chest as he lowered his head and kissed her long and deep. His tongue cut a path through her sweet mouth while his hands closed over her butt, pulling her against his erection. She leapt from the ground and wrapped her legs around his waist. Shit, she was killing him! And she had no business taking matters into her own hands. He broke the kiss and slapped her backside hard.

"Go stand over there and take your clothes off," he said curtly.

She did as she was told without arguing, reinforcing Lewis's original opinion of her as a natural sub. He searched through the bag of clothes he'd packed for her in her apartment, and found what he was looking for. He threw the garment at her.

"Put this on."

"It's too tight, Sir."

"I know. I figured it would be, which is why I packed it, just in case a situation arose. Now, never question anything either of us tells you to do. Just do it. Understood."

"Yes, Master."

He watched her as she struggled into a shocking pink Lycra mini dress that just about covered her ass, and flattened her tits against her torso. Her pebbled nipples showed clear through the fabric, crying out to be sucked and bitten. She looked like a highly fuckable slut. She looked adorable. Lewis stepped out of his shorts and tank top and threw them aside. Anais looked at him, and gasped when she saw the state of his arousal.

"Get down on your hands and knees, and come on over here."

She crawled over to him, her lovely ass poking in the air as she covered the distance that separated them. When she reached him she sat back on her haunches, and he slipped the tip of his cock into her mouth.

"Just use your mouth, babe. You need to make me harder than this if I'm to be any good to you."

Her eyes widened, like she didn't believe he could get any harder. Lewis suppressed a chuckle. She had a lot to learn. His chuckling turned to an agonized groan when she sucked him all the way into her mouth, her lips firm and arousing as she licked him thoroughly from tip to balls. Her tongue worked the sensitive underside of his cock, with immediate results. He felt himself swelling inside her mouth.

"That's it, darlin'." He thrust deep, until he hit the back of her throat. "Carry on doing that and you'll soon have my cock buried deep inside your sweet cunt." She groaned around his erection, and sucked a little harder, her cheeks hollowing out with the effort she put into it. "You really like sucking cock, don't you, sugar?" He flexed his hips, helping her along with her task. "Hmm, I could get used to this."

But he also didn't want to come in her mouth. Not this time, at any rate. He pulled out, and grinned down at her. "Stand up and spread your legs."

She did as he asked, her eyes now glittering with a combination of curiosity and desire. She sure did make a pretty picture in that tarty dress, legs wide, honey trickling down her inner thighs. He ducked his head between her legs, closed his lips over her clit, and sucked. Hard. Anais screamed and he sensed her throwing her head around as she absorbed the pleasure. He placed one hand on her backside and slid a finger between the cheeks. She tensed up, but Lewis didn't allow that to deter him. Sucking harder on her clit, and sliding a couple of fingers into her sopping cunt, he circled her anus with one finger of his other hand, sensing her relax. She was bucking her hips now, totally abandoned, forcing herself deeper into his mouth. Lewis couldn't decide whether to let her come like this, or to keep her on edge.

Making her wait won out and he abruptly abandoned what he was doing.

"Bath time," he said, chuckling at her aggrieved expression. "You have got to learn to hold back, darlin'. It's way more rewarding if you do."

"I'll take my dress off."

"No one told you to," he said, slapping her hands away from the hem when she went to pull it over her head. "Didn't Hunter make it plain that you never think for yourself when we're fucking you?"

"Yes, but—"

"Come on."

Lewis led her into the bathroom and turned on the faucets. He added a liberal amount of oil to the water, watching it foam up as he tested the temperature. When he was satisfied, he climbed into the tub and held out a hand to help her in along with him. He sat with his back to the enamel, legs splayed, and indicated to her that she should sit between them with her back to his chest. The Lycra dress clung to her damp body like a second skin, and Lewis wasted no time exploiting the situation he had created. He grabbed a sponge, soaped it and brought it around her front so he could rub it hard against her sensitized nipples. She cried out, squirming against his arousal.

"You like that, darlin'?"

"Yes, Master. It's very…err, stimulating."

"Hmm, you sure do look pretty in that dress. Lean forward on your hands and knees and let me at that butt."

Oh sweet lord, what had he set in motion, Lewis wondered. The sight of her naked pussy and cute butt just asking to be fucked was severely messing with his self-control. The Lycra had ridden right up to the top of her thighs, making her more tempting than if she'd been wearing nothing at all. Lewis grabbed a loofa and rubbed it briskly between her legs, sawing it across the lips of her pussy until she clenched around it and cried out.

"Oh no you don't!" Lewis threw the loofa aside and tapped her butt hard. "You don't get to come until I say you can."

She moaned, and threw her head around, damp hair hanging all over her face, concealing it from his view. He didn't need to see her expression to know she was severely frustrated, just the way he wanted her to be. He reached for a long-handled back brush, turned it around and slipped the handle straight into her cunt. She clearly hadn't expected it, and gasped.

"Don't move," he said curtly, getting to his knees behind her and sliding his cock up and down the crack in her butt as he continued to work the brush handle in and out of her. "If you wanna play with Hunter and me, you're gonna have to let us fuck your ass sooner or later, darlin', and trust me, it will drive you wild."

Her body was trembling, and a series of increasingly frantic little moans slipped past her lips. Lewis reached over the edge of the bath to where he'd dumped his shorts, delved into the pocket and extracted a bandana he'd had the foresight to bring with him.

"I need to see you in that slutty dress *and* gagged," he said. "Open your mouth for me, darlin'.""

She did so and he tied the bandana securely in place.

"Take a look in the mirror," he ordered. "See how hot you look."

She glanced sideways, tossed her hair out of her eyes, and he thought he heard another gasp get past her gag.

"Yeah, that's you, honey. It's the wild you who's been kept under lock and key all these years. Hunter and I will enjoy letting you out." He reached for his shorts again, found a foil packet and quickly suited up. "Okay, darlin', keep watching."

He removed the brush from her cunt and slapped her butt with the back of it several times. She gamely held her position, and he could see she was enjoying herself. One hand reached for a pert breast and tweaked the nipple hard through the wet fabric of her dress. She circled her head and barely audible sounds again got past the gag.

"We are gonna have so much fun with you, sugar. Just wait until you see our playroom downstairs."

Lewis grabbed her hips and pulled her down onto his cock. He slid straight into her without bothering to part her folds and go gently. He didn't want gentle. Nor, it seemed, did she. He held her on top of him and worked her from beneath, driven crazy by the sight of her gagged, wearing a wet Lycra dress. *Hunter should be here to enjoy the show.*

"Don't move, darlin'. Keep completely still and let me work that sweet cunt of yours."

She nodded and Lewis drove into her hard, filling her completely. She was so goddamned tight it was near killing him. He pushed a button on the side of the bath that made the water churn, just the way he was churning inside. He sensed her clenching his cock with the muscles in her vagina and knew she couldn't contain her orgasm for much longer.

"Don't you dare come," he whispered, gouging harshly at one of her nipples, ensuring that she disobeyed him.

Her body spasmed wildly and Lewis fucked her as hard and deep as he could, determined she would never forget their first time together. Her orgasm went on for what seemed like forever. He could see the wildness in her eyes when he glanced in the mirror, and knew she was having trouble believing what was happening to her. Her pleasure communicated itself to Lewis, and he had a hard job holding back—hard being the operative word. He couldn't remember the last time he'd been so big, so rock solid, so ready to detonate like an incendiary device.

He fell back on the discipline that had made him such an effective Dom and let her ride out her orgasm before he really started to move inside her again.

"That's it, sweetheart." He pushed the wet hair away from her neck and bit at it. "Now we're gonna do that again, but this time I'm coming with you. Are you ready for the ride of your life?"

She nodded. Lewis grabbed her hips and forced her down onto his throbbing cock, ramming it into her like a man on a mission. He felt something other than the raging lust that normally gripped him in such situations. He felt a deep oneness for the gorgeous creature riding his throbbing dick and didn't think he'd ever get enough of her. This was different than all the occasions that had preceded it—Anais was special and he couldn't imagine walking away from her when this assignment was over. That had never happened to him before. There was just something about her that set her apart, and Lewis wanted to make her understand that in the only way he knew how.

He felt the familiar constriction in his groin as his balls pulled tight and he again reached for Anais's tits. The white-hot explosion building inside of him couldn't remain internalized, especially when her moans managed to escape the gag, further firing his lust. Tugging at her nipples, the flickering heat turning into a raging inferno. He bit down hard on her shoulder and let rip.

"Here it comes, darlin'. We're fucking hard. Come with me, sweetheart. I want to feel you come for me again."

She gurgled behind the gag and, helpless against the raging force of his need, they fell over the edge of the cliff at the exact same moment.

"Shit, baby, you are something else." Lewis gasped as his sperm showered into the condom and Anais continued to thrash about on top of him like a woman with a point to prove to herself.

Chapter Seven

Hunter chuckled to himself as he drove off to meet with Mike Pearson. He had told Hunter on the phone that he was happy to talk to him, but was on duty at noon so Hunter needed to make him his first interview. But that wasn't what amused him. In fact, Hunter barely spared Pearson a thought. He'd size the man up once they were face to face and get the measure of him then. He would know in a heartbeat if he was being honest, or holding something back regarding Gary Harrison.

His laughter was directed at Lewis, and his expression when Hunter left him alone with Anais. He didn't need to be psychic to figure out what they would be doing right about now. Having satisfied himself that Anais had no regrets, that in fact she was eager to carry on with what they'd started the night before, he was happy to leave the field free for his buddy. Anais needed to be indoctrinated carefully into their lifestyle, and if Hunter had hung around to watch he wasn't sure he would have been able to keep away from the action. No, better to let Lewis have some fun, and they'd take it from there later. The things Hunter had planned once he got her into their playroom kept his blood pumping. He'd never indoctrinated a sub before. All the women they usually played with knew the score. Finding one who didn't, but who was so eager to learn, was a real turn-on.

Hunter's chuckles turned to groans as memories of being inside Anais caused his cock to harden and press painfully against the denim of his jeans.

"Jeez, get a grip," he said aloud.

If he turned up to interview a serving soldier with a hard-on, Pearson would probably take it personally and throw a punch at him. With this sobering thought in mind, Hunter's tumescence subsided just as he found the address he was looking for in a small residential street in downtown Tampa. He pulled into the driveway behind a spit-shiny SUV. The small property had definitely seen better days, and wore its air of neglect like a comfort blanket. An ancient tress gave the front of the house shade, Spanish moss trailing like mist from its branches. The yard was neatly kept and an effort had clearly been made to make the best of this down-market rental, its precise neatness telling Hunter a lot about the man he was about to meet.

Hunter stepped onto a wooden deck that creaked beneath his weight and found himself shaded by a porch. The front door opened before he could ring the bell. Pearson was trim, probably about forty, with thinning buzz-cut hair and probing eyes that took their time assessing Hunter. Hunter nodded as he returned the favor.

"I'm Hunter Griffin," he said, sticking out a hand. "Thanks for agreeing to see me at such short notice."

"I thought you were still serving," he said, his eyes lingering on Hunter's ponytail as he shook hands with him. "I guess not."

"No, I got out a few years back."

"Very wise."

"Yeah, all the fun had gone out of it but you don't need me to tell you that once a soldier…"

"I hear you. It kinda gets into your blood." Pearson chuckled as he pulled the door open wider and ushered Hunter inside. "I figured you were another of those investigators, coming to ask the same damned fool questions I've already answered a dozen times."

"No, like I told you on the phone. I work for Mrs. Harrison. She's keen to know what happened to her husband."

Pearson shrugged. "She and half the army, seems like, but I don't think there's much I can tell you that you probably don't already know."

"Nor can the military." Hunter had already picked up on Pearson's disillusionment and ran with it, hoping to get Pearson on his side. "She's being stonewalled by them."

"Doesn't surprise me. That's what they do best, even when there's no reason to keep quiet."

"Amen to that."

Pearson led Hunter into a spotlessly clean, impersonal lounge, the furniture almost certainly part of the rental, no feminine touches in sight. Pearson clearly lived alone. It was so sterile that Hunter briefly wondered if Pearson actually spent any time in the place. It wasn't that there wasn't a cup or newspaper out of place. There *were* no cups, papers or any signs of normal life in evidence, taking military precision—some might say anal retentiveness—to the extreme.

"Take a load off." Pearson gestured to a chair. "Can I get you anything?"

Hunter shook his head. "I know you have to report for duty, so I won't keep you long. Just a few questions."

"Shoot." Pearson took the chair opposite Hunter's. "Mrs. Harrison is a nice lady. I met her a couple of times at the base, and it must be hard for her not knowing. I'm happy to tell you what I know, but it's precious little."

"Okay, I gather you were one of four instructors conducting a two day survival course in the 'Glades."

"Right. Harrison was the sergeant in charge."

"So, when he ignored standing orders and decided to do spot-checks on the trainees alone, none of you could argue that decision?"

"Right again. When he went missing and the shit hit the fan, we all got put on report for doing what he ordered us to, which was ignoring standing orders and letting him do what the fuck he liked. If we hadn't, Harrison would have found a reason to put *us* on report." Pearson shook his head. "Can you believe that?"

Hunter could. "Tell me about Harrison. What was he like?"

"Damned good at survival, that I can tell you, and he knew it. An excellent shot, an instinctive stalker, and tough as nails."

"But you didn't like him?"

Pearson's head shot up. "That obvious, is it?"

"Pretty much."

"If you want the truth, you won't find anyone in the training sector who had a good word to say for him. 'Arrogant son of a bitch' doesn't begin to cover it. He hated being taken off active service—"

"Do you know why he was?"

"No, but he had a short fuse. He got into confrontations with several other soldiers just because they pissed him off."

"Were the incidents reported?"

Pearson shook his head. "That I couldn't say. All I do know is, he hated working with us. He thought it was beneath him, and took it out on the trainees. He gave them hell, especially if they showed the slightest signs of weakness." He spread his hands. "Shit, you know how it is, anyone who makes it through to selection for SOCOM has to be pretty tough, but we all have personal hang ups. Even the hardest guys can fall to pieces at the sight of a snake, heights, enclosed spaces or whatever, but Harrison wouldn't cut any of them any slack at all."

"He was a bully?"

"You better believe it. If you had a fear of snakes, you'd be advised to keep it to yourself because if Harrison got wind of it, you can imagine what happened. Trust me, you won't find anyone at the base who has a good word to say for him."

"He was a loner then?"

"Yeah. He never talked about his personal life to us. In fact he never talked to us at all unless it was to bark out orders about the course."

Hmm, Hunter was starting to get a bad feeling about Harrison. He would need to ask Raoul if he could get sight of his disciplinary record. If he had a temper he couldn't control, then he might well have been removed from active duty because he'd somehow screwed up something delicate. There again, the temper might be a result of having been removed unfairly from the front line.

"What was he like in the 'Glades?"

"Fucking ace, I'll give him that much. He could move as stealthily as a cat, shoot the eyes out of a target most people couldn't even see, could live a month in the wilds without breaking a sweat…a real fucking Tarzan." Pearson shook his head. "Gotta admire his skills. Shame about his personality."

"So you don't think a gator got him?"

"Not a chance. Besides, I was the one who found his rifle. That ground was completely undisturbed. I tried to tell the investigators that it would be all kicked up, and there would have been more blood, but they seemed to think they knew better."

"Okay, so what's your theory? What do you think happened to him?"

"Hell if I know." Person shrugged. He either really didn't have a theory, or wasn't about to share it. "All I can tell you is, his wife's the only one who feels his loss."

"Okay, just one last question. Do you have any idea where Harrison was deployed before he was taken off active service?"

"No, we're not allowed to discuss stuff like that, as you well know."

"Yes, but there might have been a clue. Something he said in passing about places he'd visited."

"Not him. Trappist monks could have taken lessons from him."

"Okay, well I guess that about covers it. Oh, just one more question. Ever come across a Major Dixon?"

"He's a big gun in the military police. Doesn't get involved in day-to-day investigations. Why? Is he looking for Harrison? If he is, then there's definitely something suspect about his disappearance."

That's what Hunter had supposed. "Thanks for your time." Hunter stood up and shook Pearson's hand again. "I appreciate it."

"No problem. I hope the lady finds closure." As Pearson opened the front door for Hunter, he paused with his hand on it. "Oh, one thing I just thought of. It might not mean anything, but one day I was near him, he didn't know I was there, and I heard him talking on his cell phone. Well not talking, but arguing, or that's what it sounded like, which is probably why for once he didn't detect my presence. He was preoccupied."

"You say it sounded as though he was arguing? Couldn't you tell for sure?"

"No, because he was speaking fluent Spanish and I only caught one word in ten. I didn't want him to think I was eavesdropping. I don't mind admitting the guy scared the shit out of me, and I don't frighten easily. There was just something about his eyes. They reminded me of a dead fish."

"Spanish? Hmm, well thanks, I'll check that out. Did you hear him mention any names?"

"No, sorry."

"Well, that would have been too good to be true."

Hunter got back into his truck, deep in thought. He believed what Pearson had told him, and it cast Harrison in a very different light to the picture Anais had painted of him. But then again, she was his wife, not his subordinate, and she had said he was pretty self-contained even before he started to withdraw from her. He put a quick call through to Raoul before driving off, telling him what he'd learned.

"Can you get Harrison's disciplinary records for me?" he asked.

Raoul snorted. "Do eagles soar?"

"Yeah, okay." Hunter grinned into the phone, enjoying insulting Raoul's clandestine capabilities. "The thing is, I don't peg Harrison as the sort to have had a personality transplant overnight. He might have been pissed to be removed from the front line, I get that part, but he was a real bastard to the trainees and a person doesn't suddenly turn into a sadist because of a bad career move." Hunter should know.

"I need to know where he was posted, and what he was working on before being put on training," Hunter reminded his boss.

"I'm on it, buddy."

"Catch you later."

Hunter ended the call and drove back towards the beach for his next appointment, wondering if Regan's account would jibe with Pearson's. Regan lived in a small apartment complex, situated around a swimming pool, in a quiet street several back from the beach. Fallen palm fronds littered the communal grounds and looked as though they had been there for a while. Two women on sunbeds beside the pool were both smoking. Hunter parked in a visitor's spot and rang the bell for unit four on the ground floor, conscious of the sunbathers giving him a thorough onceover. He was taken aback when a guy in a wheelchair opened the door to him. He knew Regan had been invalided out of the service. He hadn't realized he was physically handicapped.

"Don't worry," the guy said, grinning at Hunter. "You should see the other guy."

They shook hands, and Hunter immediately took to Regan. "What happened?" he asked as he followed the wheelchair into a studio room, which was the entire apartment, small but ideal for wheelchair access. "Although you must get sick of answering that question."

"MS. That's why I was taken off active duty and given a training post. It was supposed to be under control, I was supposed to have a couple more years before I got to this stage but, as you can see, shit happens."

"I'm sorry."

"Don't be. It ain't your fault. Besides, I'm resigned to it. Can I get you anything?"

"No, I'm good, thanks. I just wanted to ask you about Harrison."

Regan spun his chair on the spot until he faced the seat Hunter had taken, his jovial expression replaced by a frown. "That bastard ain't no loss."

"Glad you don't feel the need to hold back," Hunter replied, chuckling.

"Sorry, but you won't find anyone with a good word to say about him. He was a mean, sadistic bastard, and that's on a good day."

"You sound as though you're talking from experience."

Regan grimaced. "Trust me, I am. I didn't ask for any quarter because of my condition, and was prepared to pull my weight. I knew my limitations, so did the army, that's why they put me on training duties. I had regular check-up with the squad's medics, still had use of my legs, and was fit for the duties prescribed to me. But Harrison didn't agree. He said he wasn't prepared to carry deadwood. Called me a cripple, a waste of space, and a few other labels I won't offend your ears by repeating."

Hunter grimaced. "Sounds like a real charmer."

"You have no idea." Regan spread his hands. "And it wasn't just me. He picked on weaknesses in everyone he came across and exploited them, just to make him appear like a tough guy."

"You're not the first person to tell me that."

"Look, I'm sorry for his wife's loss, but she can do a hell of a lot better than Harrison."

Hunter privately agreed. He quizzed Regan for another quarter of an hour but didn't learn anything he hadn't already gotten from Pearson.

"Do you happen to know if Harrison spoke Spanish?"

"No, I never heard him if he did, but then why would I? Is it important?"

"Not necessarily." Hunter stood up. "You seem pretty self-sufficient here."

"I am, and I intend to stay that way just as long as I can."

Hunter liked and respected Regan more by the minute. "Do you still drive?"

"Yeah." He pointed to a converted van parked outside his condo. "It's amazing the advances made with transport for people like me nowadays." He sniffed. "Call me a cynic, but it probably means less expenditure on care if we can get about on our own."

Hunter laughed. "You're probably right about that."

"Well, anyway, if there's anything I can do to help Mrs. Harrison find closure you have but to say the word. My agenda ain't especially packed with appointments nowadays."

Hunter sensed that was as close as Regan was likely to come to sounding sorry for himself.

"Thanks." Regan wheeled himself to the front door and opened it. Hunter shook his hand. "I'll bear that in mind."

As Hunter drove back home, several thoughts flickered through his mind. If there was a grain of truth in any of them, he was starting to understand why the military was getting so paranoid about this case. There were now a number of creditable theories regarding Harrison's disappearance. He could have fallen foul of whoever he'd been arguing with. Anais said his personality changed once he came off active duties, possibly because he was under some sort of disciplinary cloud. But could it be that he'd made as many enemies outside the service as he appeared to have done within it, and one or more of them had used his presence in the 'Glades to make him disappear? Didn't seem likely, not if Harrison was as tough and resourceful as his subordinates grudgingly conceded.

Another possibility was that Gary Harrison had staged his own disappearance for reasons Hunter had yet to uncover. Or his subordinates had had enough of his bully-boy tactics and done the world a favor.

All Hunter knew for sure was that his disappearance had been no accident. And unless the military investigators had developed a collective case of stupidity since Hunter's day, then they knew it, too.

Chapter Eight

"Hey, how did it go?" Lewis looked up from his computer when Hunter entered their study.

"Interesting. Where's Anais?"

"Sleeping." Lewis smirked. "She had a hard morning."

Hunter grinned in response. "You guys have fun?"

"And then some." Lewis closed his eyes, threw back his head and sighed. "She's something else, man."

"Yeah, she is."

"Why did you say it like that?" Lewis's eyes flow open. "What are you thinking? About her, I mean."

"Probably the same thing you are. I haven't been in this position since...well, since forever. But first things first. We need to figure out what happened to her husband."

"That we do. So tell me."

Hunter perched his butt on the edge of his desk and told Lewis everything he'd learned, finishing up with the conclusions he'd drawn.

"We need to know where he went overseas," Lewis said, stating the obvious.

"Raoul's already on it, but I have my suspicions."

"On what?" Anais stood in the doorway.

"Hey, babe. You feeling rested?" Hunter threw an arm around her shoulders and held her against him. "This oaf didn't wear you out?"

She giggled. "That oaf was a lot of fun."

"See." Lewis treated Hunter to another smug grin.

"Okay, let's go in the other room where we can be more comfortable, then I'll let you both in on what I found out today." Well, in Anais's case, some of it. "You hungry, darlin'? Want some lunch?"

"No, thanks." She patted her belly. "I'm still full of all that breakfast you made me eat."

"Yeah, I forced it down your neck." Hunter twitched her nose as he led her from the room. "Tell you what, we'll make do with coffee for now, then we'll have dinner early, and after that—"

"Yes?" Lewis and Anais asked together, sending Hunter identical expectant looks.

"Well, if you're a real bad girl, and if you don't feel like we're rushing you, we might take your education a step farther."

Her smile was broad and infectious. "How bad do I need to be?"

Both men laughed. "The badder the better."

"I'll fix the coffee," Lewis said, heading for the kitchen.

While he did so, Hunter sat with Anais, took her hand in his and told her what he'd heard about her husband. "It doesn't jibe with what you said about him, darlin'."

"No, but I saw a different side to him. I knew him from school, remember."

"But you said he changed, became more distant," Lewis reminded her as he rejoined them with coffee and cookies on a tray.

"True, but I figured he was pissed at having to be what he called a babysitter for the recruits."

"Some babies," Lewis replied. "The troops chosen for SOCOM are no pussycats."

"I know, but—"

"I should have asked you this before," Hunter said. "Gary's car, what happened to it?"

"It was in the garage of our house on the base. He didn't need it the day he left because he was off to the Everglades."

"That's what I figured. Presumably the investigators looked over it."

She nodded. "They didn't find anything, that much I do know." Anais frowned. "What are you thinking, Hunter?"

Hunter recalled seeing something about a negative search of a personal vehicle in the report Raoul hacked into. "Did he have access to other vehicles?"

"My car, but I had that with me."

"One more thing, darlin'. Did you know he spoke fluent Spanish?"

Anais widened her eyes. "I knew he had a working knowledge of the language. A lot of SOCOM people do, but I was unaware he was fluent." She frowned. "Are you sure?"

"Pearson heard him on the phone to someone."

She shook her head. "It just goes to show. You never really know a person, even when you think you do."

"Are you absolutely sure he didn't have any personal friends we don't know about?"

"This time yesterday I would have been positive. Now I feel as though I didn't know the man I was married to at all." She paused, her expression reflective. "You think he did something bad to make his disappearance happen, don't you?"

Lewis poured the coffee and handed the mugs around. "We don't know what to think yet, babe. We're still trying to piece it all together."

"If I'm right, it's probably why the military stonewalled me?"

"That's my guess." Hunter squeezed the hand he was still holding in his. "Don't let it get to you. We'll get to the bottom of it. It's what we do."

She regarded him through eyes that suddenly seemed too large for her face. "Do you think he was killed, murdered, for some reason?"

"I'm not discounting any possibilities, darlin'. I won't lie to you about that."

"Don't lie to me about anything. I would prefer to know what you're thinking. Don't try to protect me."

"Wouldn't think of it." Lewis winked at her as he snagged a cookie, lightening the mood with his irreverence.

"If you want to know the truth, our relationship had been on the slide for over a year before Gary disappeared."

Both men sat straighter in their seats.

"That's not what you said before," Hunter replied, his tone one of mild reproof. "You gave us the impression that everything was good until Gary was forced into the training unit."

"Well, it's hard to be honest about your feelings when you think your husband died while serving his country. It would have felt disloyal. But now...well, I don't know what to think. Perhaps I always knew there was something odd about his disappearance but wasn't ready to face it before now."

"When did things start to go wrong between you guys?"

Anais screwed up her eyes. "It's hard to put a precise date on it. I guess we were on a slow downward spiral, same as a lot of military marriages, because of the strain of separations, the risks the men take, living with the very real possibility of being killed and...well, I don't need to tell you how it is." Both men nodded. "He was always tense and uncommunicative, especially when he came back from assignments, and it took him a while to get back to normal. About a year before he was removed from active duty he came home one time and was even worse. The first thing he always wanted to do was...well, you know." She blushed. "But not this time. He treated me like I didn't exist, moved into the spare room without explaining why, wouldn't talk to me about it, and we never shared a bed again."

"I know it's hard for you to talk about personal stuff, but you still should have told us before now, darlin'," Hunter said softly.

"Well, I'm telling you now, but I don't see how it's relevant."

"It tells us a lot," Lewis replied. "Given what we now know, it's safe to assume that whatever ate at him, happened while he was on active duty."

"Presumably somewhere they speak Spanish." Hunter suspected he and Lewis were thinking the same thing, but out of deference for Anais's bruised feelings, didn't put those thoughts into words. "Okay, it's time to look at your records of Gary's cell phone calls."

"I'll go get the laptop."

Lewis sprang athletically to his feet and returned a short time later with the computer. He set it up on the coffee table in front of Anais and sat on the other side of her from Hunter. They spent the next hour going through the numbers Gary had called. There weren't many of them. The base, an outdoor supplier, a gun club, his bank.

"Nothing suspicious at all," Hunter said. "Although we might want to visit the outdoor supplier. If he staged his own disappearance, he would have needed stuff."

Anais gasped. "Do you really think he did that?"

"I have absolutely no idea, but we can't afford to discount the possibility."

Anais shook her head. "Why would he? If he'd found someone else—"

"If he had, there would be calls, but it doesn't sound like he made any effort with women." Lewis patted her hand. "Why would he when he had you to come home to. Anyway, no one mentioned seeing him with a woman, either today or in the report we read."

"He was good looking, and could be charming when he put his mind to it," Anais said. "Women liked him."

"But he didn't return their interest?" Hunter suggested.

"No, he always said I was the only one for him."

"We'd best take a look at his e-mail," Lewis said. "There's nothing here to lend us any clues."

"There's not much to see." Anais pulled up his account. "He wasn't one for computers. He never really trusted them. Said they were too easy to hack into."

Hunter thought of Raoul's sophisticated hacking abilities and grinned. "He had a point."

"I've never known anyone to be so self-contained," Lewis complained when Gary's e-mail account yielded no new clues. "Almost no phone calls, no e-mail, no friends. The guy's a fucking phantom." He glanced at Anais and grimaced. "Sorry, babe, but it's just not natural in this day and age."

"No apology necessary. I'd be the first to admit that he was a bit different. When you live with it all the time different starts to seem normal."

They turned their attention to Gary's bank account, which was equally uninformative. No large deposits or withdrawals, no suspicious activities, and no activity at all since the date of his disappearance.

"Okay, we've got all we're going to get from here," Hunter said, standing up and stretching. "I'll go and get dinner started."

"Let me help," Anais offered.

They ate an hour later. Hunter kept Anais busy in the kitchen in the meantime, chatting to her about things that had nothing to do with her husband. He could see she was distracted by the discussion they'd just had—she would have to be made of stone not to be, and Hunter had good reason to know she was all warm flesh and blood. He hated seeing her hurt and bewilderment in her eye, but saw little point in sugar-coating his findings. Her husband wasn't the man she thought he had been, could well still be alive, and was almost certainly the subject of a military enquiry that was being kept under wraps.

His kitchen was usually strictly his domain, but he enjoyed having Anais in it with him. She worked quietly and efficiently, and didn't get in his way. Hunter, on the other hand, found excuses to bump his body against hers. Just because her husband was stupid enough to neglect her, that didn't mean she wasn't *the* most sensuous, feisty, desirable woman he'd met in years of searching. Gary Harrison was a jerk, but Hunter and Lewis were more than capable of appreciating Anais's feminine qualities, and letting her know it.

The atmosphere was rife with expectancy as they ate their dinner. Anais ate quickly and sparingly, as though she couldn't wait to find out what came next. The guys taunted her by eating slowly, pretending they didn't know what it was that had gotten her so excited.

"We'll take dessert in the other room," Hunter eventually said, having cleared away the plates. "Come with us."

He held out a hand and Anais slipped hers into it. Lewis walked ahead of them and opened the door that led directly into the room behind their garage. He flipped on the low lights set in the baseboard that sent arcs of illumination over the crimson walls of their dungeon. He watched for Anais's reaction. It wasn't long in coming. She looked around at the array of BDSM playthings—spanking benches, whips, toys, a large water bed, and numerous appliances she probably didn't have a clue how to use, and gasped.

"What is this place?" she asked.

* * * *

She knew, of course, even though she had never imagined she would set foot in one. She felt incredibly excited. So too did her leaking pussy. She hadn't admitted it, even to herself, but she had felt hurt and humiliated by Gary's withdrawal from her. She knew from other military wives that their men often felt detached from reality, and found it hard to settle back to a normal life after a difficult or dangerous posting. Gary had always bounced back in the past, but each time he did so he offered less of himself, treating her increasingly like a stranger. And then the ultimate insult of insisting upon separate rooms. She had felt it was her fault because she must have failed to give him the support he needed.

Now she was starting to think differently.

These two gorgeous specimens of unimpeachable masculinity wanted her just for herself. There was no question this was a mercy fuck. She knew she was responsible for taking their relationship to this level, and it hadn't been their intention. They had this cute sense of propriety and she was pretty sure they didn't make a habit out of mixing business with pleasure. *Get used to it, boys. I like your games.*

"This is our playroom, darlin'," Hunter said, bending his head to steal a kiss. "And you're a very welcome addition to it."

"What sort of games do you play in here?" she asked, licking her lips because they were suddenly very dry, and because she liked the way Hunter always seemed to tense up whenever she did it.

"Not any that require clothing. Take your things off, sweetheart, all of them."

Both men stood back and watched her as she stripped for them. She did so slowly, glad she'd bothered to wear a matching lacy bra and pantie set. Not that they got to see her in it for long, but still. When she was naked, she looked up at them, waiting to be told what to do next.

"Put a plastic sheet on the bed," Hunter told Lewis. "Then go get the bowl of whipped cream and fruit from the fridge. We're gonna eat our dessert from a very desirable table."

Lewis grinned, blew Anais a kiss, flipped a thin-looking plastic sheet over the mattress and slipped back out the door.

"Go and lay on the bed."

Hunter looked his fill at Anais as he spoke, but didn't touch her. She so wanted him to touch her that she couldn't prevent her body from trembling all over. He appeared not to notice, but the tight little smile he clearly didn't want her to see gave him away, lending Anais confidence. She lay on the bed and looked away from him, glad he wasn't indifferent to her nakedness. It really mattered to her that she should make an impression upon him—upon them both. When she looked up again, Hunter was also naked. And aroused. Oh my, very aroused! Yep, that was what she called making an impression.

"You sure do look pretty like that, darlin'. Lift your arms above your head and spread your legs just as wide as you can get them."

She wasn't surprised when he cuffed her wrists and fastened the chain connecting them to the bedhead. But she was astonished when he produced restraints from beneath the bed and fastened them around her ankles, securing them in place.

"There, now there's no escape for you."

Who wants to escape?

Lewis returned, minus his clothes, but clutching the large bowl of soft fruit and cream she had seen in the fridge earlier.

"Now ain't that the prettiest sight you ever did see," Lewis said, admiration in his tone.

"No question," Hunter agreed. "You hungry, buddy?"

"I could use some dessert."

A large dollop of cream fell on Anais's midriff, making her squirm. Except she couldn't move very much because her limbs were secured in place. Now she understood why. Further dollops landed on her tits, and her pussy. Oh my, were they going to lick it off? Please lick it off, she silently begged. Hunter climbed onto the bed beside her and held a spoon of fruity cream to her lips. She extended her tongue and lapped it up like a cat. The mattress, a water-filled mattress, she realized now, dipped at the bottom as Lewis clambered between her legs. Without preamble, he dipped his tongue into her cream-covered pussy and sucked it up. Anais elevated her hips from the bed and moaned. She simply couldn't help herself, the sensation was so intense, so mind-numbingly electrifying. Hunter dropped his head and bit hard at a solidified nipple as he ate the cream from her tits, at which point Anais decided she must have died and gone to heaven.

On and on it went. Their tongues and teeth were everywhere. Anais cried out when she felt Lewis's hand filling her pussy with fistfuls of cream. It felt alien, and yet sexy as hell as it started to ooze out of her again. She fervently hoped he planned to ram it deeper with his cock. How erotic would that be? Anais had never even imagined such a thing, much less though it could happen to her. Now she couldn't wait to get started. Her prayers were answered when she heard a foil packet rip open. Then Lewis was inside her, squishing the cream deeper with firm upward thrusts of his hips.

"Your turn to feed, darlin'."

Anais turned her head sideways toward the voice. She was confronted by Hunter, on his knees beside her face, fisting his enormous cock covered with fruit and cream. A wide smile broke across her face as she opened her mouth and sucked him inside, keen to return just a fraction of the pleasure these guys had so far given her.

"That's it, baby," Hunter said with a groan. "You've got Lewis fucking your cunt, and me fucking your lovely mouth, but I'm betting it still ain't enough for you."

Hunter held his cock at its base and forced it in and out of her mouth, setting his own rhythm, hitting the back of her throat with every sortie even though she wasn't getting his entire length. Jeez, there was a lot of him, but Anais wasn't complaining.

"She'll never get enough," Lewis said, making it sound like a complaint as, breathing heavily, he rammed himself into her. She felt juices pouring out of her, unsure whether they were her own or if they were made by the cream, not especially caring because the feeling was so intoxicatingly sensual it stoked her growing need. Being fucked by two such virile guys had all her synapses firing. It was almost as though her entire life had been building up to this moment, and she never wanted it to end.

But she knew it was about to. The feel of Lewis's cock stretching the walls of her cunt, Hunter's thick length growing larger, pulsating more violently inside her mouth, and the desire pooling deliciously in her core was an incendiary combination. Fire lanced through her veins and she mewled around Hunter's cock, thrashing her body as much as she was able against the restraints. Shivers of liquid excitement stoked the flames. She was on the brink, and wouldn't be able to pull back now, no matter what threats they issued.

"I think our little sub is getting ideas above herself," Hunter said, feeding himself between her lips with added urgency.

Lewis increased the pressure of his downward slides, setting up a hot, sticky tempo. "Looks that way."

"Course, if she comes without our permission, she'll have to be punished afterward."

"Goes without being said. What do you have in mind for her?"

"Seems to me we've ignored that cute butt of hers for quite long enough."

Anais momentarily tensed at the thought of anal sex, then relaxed again. She knew she could safe word them if it got too much, but so far everything they'd done to her hadn't been nearly enough and she was still hungry for more. Besides, she couldn't think about anything except the quite exquisite feel of Lewis's cock splitting her in two. Being spoken about like she wasn't there while they continued to fuck her was a total turn-on. Anais felt her pulse quicken as sensation, palpable and pulsating, coursed through her heated blood. She closed her vagina muscles around Lewis's cock and her mouth around Hunter's, enjoying his addictive scent and the quite devastating taste of him. Shards of pleasure blasted her body as she milked Lewis's cock, sucked harder at Hunter's, and rode the crest of her orgasm as it hit her like an erupting volcano. She gloried in the power of her femininity, the strength of which she was only just starting to understand, as sensation slammed her and all hell broke loose deep within her most sensitive areas.

"Naughty."

But there was laughter in Hunter's voice as he abruptly pulled his cock from her mouth, and pumped it between his fist. She watched him as he threw his head back, and face contorted with pleasure as he cried out as he shot his load over her sticky tits. At the exact same moment, Lewis pounded into her hard, the ropey muscles in his forearms trembling.

"You goddamned sexy bitch. Your cunt is so fucking tight it's killing me."

His entire body spasmed as she sensed his cock fill inside her. He groaned and let himself go.

They released her hands and feet almost immediately and the three of them lay on their backs, adhering to the sheet and to each other, waiting to recover their breath.

Chapter Nine

Hunter was the first to stir. He elevated himself up onto one elbow, leaned over Anais, and simply looked into her dazed eyes. His own eyes softened at the sight of her flushed face and sultry, satiated expression. The way she had adapted to the games they liked to play was driving him crazy, and causing him to think the unthinkable. Letting Anais go when this was over was no longer an option. But was he actually ready to *commit*?

He lowered his head and kissed her long and deep, astonished to find he didn't feel ready to run a mile like he usually did if he felt a trap closing around him. Perhaps that was because Anais had no idea what she did to him, and had no ulterior motive. But kids? She wanted kids, but they had never been in Hunter's agenda, nor Lewis's.

"Hey, you okay?" he asked when he finally let her up for air.

"A tad sticky," she replied, with an embarrassed little laugh. "But apart from that, absolutely wonderful."

"That's good to know." He trailed a finger across her torso, avoiding his sperm, already crystalizing on her tits. "We need to get cleaned up, all of us, so you can take your punishment."

"Do I deserve to be punished?"

"No question," Lewis replied from her opposite side, his fingers lazing exploring her body, too. "You need to learn to do as you're told, sugar."

"I need extra help with that." She shared a rueful smile between them. "I'm new to these games, and don't have your self-control, gentlemen."

Hunter watched her bite her lip as she spoke, a compelling habit that got to him every time and which would earn her an additional punishment. He wondered what magic she was working on him. Never had a woman fascinated him so comprehensively. He had thought he was too jaded to feel this way ever again, and the intense, gravitational pull that drew him to Anais almost frightened him. He had plenty of the self-control she claimed to lack as a general rule, except when he was anywhere near her, it seemed.

"That's because you've never been fucked by two men at once before." Hunter drew lazy patterns around the sparkling ruby stud in her pierced belly button with his forefinger. "You'll soon learn, and we'll be happy to teach you."

"Hmm, if you say so, Sir, but I have a feeling it will take a ton more lessons before I get the hang of it."

Hunter laughed, slapped her thigh hard, and then got up to set the shower in the corner of the dungeon running. Lewis helped her up and the three of them got themselves clean. It was clear Anais was hoping for action in the shower, but Hunter had other plans for her.

They got her dry and then told her to go stand in the corner with her back to them. She obeyed without creating problems, eyes downcast. Hunter didn't need to look into them to know they would be burning with a mixture of curiosity and excitement. The guys got themselves dry, and Lewis whipped the soiled plastic sheet from the bed.

"What you got in mind?" he asked Hunter in an undertone.

"Her ass is mine."

"Yeah, I got that part." Lewis grinned. "Think I don't know what you like after all this time?"

Hunter chuckled. "Just staking first claim, is all."

"Okay, but we need to punish her first. Think she can take a whipping?"

They both glanced at Anais's naked back and noticed a quiver pass through her body. She couldn't possibly be cold, so it had to have been caused by anticipation, or excitement because she would know they were talking about her, deciding her fate.

"I think that's what she's hoping for." Hunter reached for a Japanese flogger and cracked it across his palm. The whistle made by the thongs as they cut through the air caused Anais to flinch. "Get some clamps for her tits," he said to Lewis.

Lewis grinned. "I'm on it."

"Come over here, Anais," Hunter said when Lewis had the clamps ready.

She turned and walked slowly toward them, eyes still downcast. Hunter noticed fresh juices trickling from her cunt. She was turned on again, ready for more fun. She stopped in front of them, saying nothing. Lewis reached forward and tenderly applied lube to one solidified nipple. Then he attached a clamp. She gasped and briefly looked up, unmistakable passion reflected in her eyes. They didn't need to ask if the clamp hurt. It was obvious she loved the feel of it, and so Lewis repeated the process with the other nipple, and tugged gently at the chain that connected them when he was done. This time she moaned, and then shifted her position so her legs were wider apart. The minx was hoping for some attention to her cunt. Well, that wasn't on the agenda.

"Come with me."

Hunter led the way across the floor and stopped by a spanking bench. "On your knees, lean your torso over the bench, and let your tits dangle free on the other side."

Once she was in position, Lewis slid beneath her onto a soft gym mat, so his mouth was level with her tits. Hunter stood behind her, flexing the flogger, enjoying the sight of her cute butt just waiting for him to do whatever the hell he felt like with it. And he would. But first he needed to whip her, and put some color into those sweet buttocks.

"This is to be your punishment for coming without permission, Anais. Do you have something to say to me?"

"Yes, Sir. Please punish me. I deserve it."

"What did you do that was wrong?"

"I had an orgasm."

"And why was that wrong?"

"Because you didn't give me permission to come, Sirs."

"Damned straight we didn't. You have to learn not to disobey us."

Hunter brought the flogger down on her backside hard without giving her any warning. The multi-thongs spread the sting, leaving a pretty pink trail in their wake. She cried out, but gamely held her position. Lewis would be giving her clamped tits attention at the same time, and Hunter could see his fingers playing with her clit. Pleasure and pain. Yin and yang. Anais was already a convert, and seemed to know how to control her breathing in order to get the most of out her punishment without them needing to instruct her. He brought the flogger down harder several times in quick succession, becoming more aroused by the minute as Anais soaked up everything he could give her as though she had been doing this for months rather than days.

"Okay, Anais. Lay on your back on the mat where Lewis just was." Lewis moved out of the way and she did as Hunter asked. "Bring your knees up and spread your legs wide."

Hunter brought the flogger down three times over her pussy. He was breathing heavily when he stopped, and his cock was twitching almost out of control.

"Have you learned your lesson, Anais?"

"Yes, Sir. Thank you for teaching me."

"Get on your hands and knees, darlin'." She hesitated for the first time, causing Hunter to raise the flogger again. "Don't make me ask twice."

She squealed and scurried into position. Hunter knelt behind her, ran his hand over her now-pink buttocks in soothing sweeps, and bent his head to gently kiss and nip at each of them in turn. Then he ran his cock down the crack between them.

"You like the feel of that, sugar?"

"I…I think so. Will it hurt?"

"No, sweet thing, it will blow your mind. Just trust me."

He lubed a finger and played with her anus. He wasn't surprised when she tensed up against him, but once again Lewis was beneath her, laying sideways on and playing with her tits, distracting her. Hunter slid a finger inside her, or tried to. He met immediate resistance, and knew he was being too gentle. He tapped a buttock and spoke severely.

"Let me in. Don't disappoint me." He felt her relax and his finger slipped past her coiled muscle. "There you go. See, it wasn't so very hard, was it?"

"No, Master. It feels kinda invasive though."

"Hmm." He bent his head again and bit her buttock, his finger still inside her, moving around, exploring. Working in perfect tandem, Lewis would be sucking her clit, or teasing her clamped nipples, or some such thing. Anais wouldn't know what to expect, or from which direction. Their deliberate ploy was to keep her turned on, guessing, waiting and, most importantly of all, wanting. "You are so frigging hot, babe."

She mumbled something as Hunter added another finger. This time she didn't fight him. In fact she wiggled her butt against his fingers. Shit, she was something else! Time to take her a stage farther. He reached for the butt plug he had in hand, lubed it up, and gently removed his fingers. Before she could readjust, he slipped the tip of the plug into her, aware that Lewis's distraction techniques would be keeping pace with his actions. She gasped as he slid the entire plug deep into her.

"How does that feel?"

"Intrusive, but kinda nice."

Hunter chuckled. "Stand up, sweetheart."

She did so, and he and Lewis took a moment to admire the view. With her pink buttocks and clamped tits, her eyes still hazy with a combination of *just fucked* and renewed passion, she looked adorable.

"Come on."

He held out a hand, which she took, and the three of them made their way back to the sitting room. He could tell by the way she walked with her buttocks squeezed together that she was worried about the plug slipping out. Hunter slid a finger into her anus when they reached the seats. It had slipped just a little so he pushed it deeper. Lewis grabbed a blanket and threw it over the settee to avoid it being stained by Anais's flowing juices.

"I expect you wonder what happens now," Hunter said.

"It's not my place to ask, Sir."

"No, it isn't, but I'm happy to tell you. That plug in your ass, darlin', is filled with oil. Your body heat will warm it up, and set you on fire. The plug with distend your ass, getting it ready for my cock. Lewis has gone to open a bottle of wine, we'll drink it, and by the time we're done, you'll be ready." He nuzzled her neck, nipping at the pulse beating out of control at the base of her throat. "Then I'm gonna fuck your sweet ass right here on the rug."

"Thank you, Sir."

Hunter chuckled. "You're entirely welcome."

Lewis returned with the wine bottle and three glasses. He poured and handed the glasses around.

"Here's to you, babe," Hunter said, raising his glass to Anais.

"I'll drink to that." Lewis raised his glass also.

"Thank you, Sirs." She took a sip, her expression reflective.

"Something on your mind?" Hunter asked.

"Yes, it's about condoms. If you'd prefer not to use them, I'm on the pill."

The guys exchanged a look. "I thought you and Gary weren't sleeping together even before he disappeared. Besides, he's been gone for two years and you said there was no one else," Hunter said, hoping she'd been honest about that, even though he had no right to expect it of her.

"True. But I was getting really bad periods, so my OBGYN suggested the pill to regulate them. It worked, so I've stuck with it."

"Well, baby," Lewis said, grinning. "If you don't mind us going bareback, we'd be more than happy to oblige. We're both clean."

"I want to feel you," she said, blushing but somehow managing to look defiant at the same time.

"Amen to that." Hunter raised his glass in another toast. "And talking of feeling, how you doing with that plug?"

She wiggled around. "Things are...err, heating up. It's astonishing."

"Hmm." Hunter blew her a kiss. "And I'm guessing it's lonely. Let's liven things up while we drink our wine. Bring your feet up onto the couch, darlin', bend your knees up and spread your thighs wide. Give us an up-close view of that cute pussy of yours."

Anais's eyes flashed with anticipation as she did as she was told. Lewis produced a large vibrator, slid it into her slick cunt and turned it on low. Then both men moved onto the settee opposite her.

"Make yourself come," Hunter said tersely. "We want to watch you."

She blinked, appearing surprised, but then a slow, sexy smile spread across her face. She moved one hand to the vibrator and started plunging it in and out of her, hard and deep.

"How does it feel against the plug?" Hunter asked.

"Like I'm absolutely full."

Hunter chuckled. "I hate to tell you this, sweet thing, but that plug ain't nearly as big as my cock."

Anais shot him a look, but quickly lowered her eyes again.

"We love watching you fucking yourself," Lewis said, his voice thick. "I could watch this particular show all day."

"It won't take all day," Hunter replied. "With a butt plug, nipple clamps and a vibrator, it'll all be over in seconds, you just wait and see."

They had lost Anais. Her eyes were closed, her head lolled to one side and her hips moved faster and faster against the vibrator. "I love having you watch me, gentlemen. I had no idea I would enjoy an audience, but it's a real turn-on."

"Tug on the nipple chain with your other hand, sweetheart," Lewis said.

She did so, and gasped. She flexed her hips faster and started to moan. "I'm going to come," she said. "It's…I, oh shit, here it is."

She rode the vibrator as her moans got louder, sounding almost tortured. She shuddered and clenched around the toy. Her face was flushed, her breathing ragged, and a light film of perspiration decorated her brow.

"Wow." She finally stilled but it was a moment before she opened her eyes again. When she did she looked embarrassed and kept her eyes lowered. She pulled the vibrator out and Lewis reached forward to take it from her. "That was awesome."

"We thought it was pretty hot, too." Hunter chuckled as he shared the last of the wine between their glasses. "Now that you've taken the edge off, I expect you to last a little longer when I fuck your ass. Is that clear?"

"I will surely try, Master Hunter," she replied, sipping at her wine.

She drank quickly, as though she couldn't wait to get it on. Hunter empathized, and drained his glass in two swallows.

"Okay, babe, on your hands and knees," he said curtly.

She whimpered, clumsy in her haste to comply. Hunter and Lewis shared a grin. She'd had two orgasms in the past hour, but was still hungry for more. Make that desperate to try something new. Hunter positioned himself behind her and administered a few sharp slaps to her backside with the flat of his hand. Lewis tugged the nipple chain at the same time, and Hunter would bet good money that her body was already going into sensual meltdown. She sure as hell wasn't complaining about their activities, so he figured it had to be.

"Just remember your safe word if it gets too much, darlin'," Hunter said.

He slid a finger into her anus, found the end of the plug and pulled it free. She moaned when it fell away, like she didn't want to part with it.

"Don't worry, sugar. I've got something here that you'll like even more. Take your weight on your forearms, angel. Lewis has got something for you to get your sweet lips around."

Hunter played with her backside while Lewis's cock made itself at home inside of her mouth. He'd be able to come that way now she'd agreed to no condoms. That thought made Hunter's cock twitch as he returned to the job in hand. He applied lube to his best friend and slid its head into her anus. Her entire body tensed up.

"It's okay, Anais, I've got you. I'll take real good care of you, honey. You've just gotta trust me."

He gently rubbed her buttocks with one hand as he eased a little deeper. This time she let him in, and Hunter gradually, very carefully, worked his way into her. She gurgled around Lewis's cock, but Hunter sensed it wasn't a sign of distress. Encouraged, he carefully thrust a little deeper, and then withdrew before repeating the process. The friction was electrifying, causing his senses to reel and his self-control to slip. Again. What the fuck was it about Anais that messed with his mind as well as his body?

"She's loving what you're doing to her ass, buddy," Lewis said. "And she's also fucking ace at giving head."

"Don't I just know it." Hunter slid a little deeper, and upped the tempo. "This is fucking heaven."

He closed his eyes and continued to work her, getting closer to the point of no return, anxious to take Anais with him. He thought she was having a good time but, for once, she didn't seem to be bursting to come. Having her masturbate had been a good idea. Problem was, he wasn't too sure, in his current state of heightened awareness, how long he could hold back and wait for her. Shit, when had that last happened to him? Hunter's staying power was legendary. He worked her ass a little less carefully, burying himself balls deep.

"That's it, sugar, you've got me all now. Come on, angel, let's fuck."

She gurgled, and a strangled cry from Lewis told Hunter his buddy was about to ejaculate.

"That's it, darling." Lewis bucked into her mouth. "You just keep doing that. It's so fucking hot. Shit, here it comes!"

Lewis let himself go, and Hunter glanced sideways so he could catch sight of Anais in profile as she desperately tried to swallow down his flow of semen. Eventually his buddy pulled out of her mouth and grinned.

"Hey, babe, you are something else."

Lewis kissed her lips, but remained where he was, ready to tantalize her while Hunter did his stuff. Anais was now hot and slick, all her attention on Hunter's cock. He grabbed her hips and ground himself into her.

"Come on then, darling, let's do this."

"Yes, it feels…it feels like I never would have imagined."

Her body trembled as Lewis tugged hard on the nipple chain. She cried out, and Hunter knew she was now ready to rock. He thrust hard, one fluid glide all it took for her to fragment. He went right along with her, holding her hips in a death grip as his groin constricted and he lost himself inside the woman he was pretty sure he'd fallen hopelessly in love with.

"Ah, sweet Anais," he said, wiping sweat from his brow when he finally stopped coming. "You blow me away. Are you okay?"

"Hmm, wonderful."

He pulled out of her, fell onto his back on the rug, and dragged her into his arms. "You are something else."

"Amen to that." Lewis joined them on the rug and took his turn to kiss her.

"Thank you," she said, smothering a yawn with the back of her hand. "I had absolutely no idea what I'd been missing all these years."

"Well, we're more than willing to help you make up for lost time," Lewis assured her as he removed the nipple clamps.

"Aw, that tingles."

"Yep." Lewis looked pleased with himself. "The clamps starve your nipples of blood. When it starts flowing again, that's the best part."

She mangled her lower lip between her teeth. "So I'm finding out."

Hunter stood up, picked her up from the floor and cradled her against his chest. "You're also finding out that energetic sex is exhausting. Come on, sweetheart, I'll take you up to bed, get you cleaned up and tucked in for the night."

"I want to sleep with you guys," she said, pouting.

"Ain't gonna happen," Hunter replied. "Not while we still have the issue of your husband to resolve."

"I don't see what difference that makes."

"It makes all the difference. If you sleep with either one of us, or both, we won't do much sleeping, and we need to keep clear heads until we get this mess cleaned up."

"Hmm. I suppose that's true, but—"

"No *buts,* darlin'. You've had enough for one day, and that's final."

Both guys went up with her. Hunter placed her in her bed, Lewis got a wash cloth and wiped her clean, then they pulled the covers up to her chin and each kissed her goodnight.

"Sleep well, babe," Hunter said, blowing her a kiss as he switched off the light and closed the door on her.

"Wow!" Lewis said as the guys made their way downstairs again.

"My thoughts exactly." Hunter headed for the study, not prepared to say anything else about Anais. Until he sorted out his own feelings, made some sort of sense of them, there was nothing he could say. "We need to see if there's anything in from Raoul," he said instead.

There was. He'd gotten hold of Gary's army records, including details of his postings.

"He'd been on report several times for losing his temper," Lewis said, reading over Hunter's shoulder.

"From what we've learned about his personality, that shouldn't come as a big surprise."

"And you were right in what you were thinking. Hiss most recent three postings have been counter-narcotics operations in Honduras."

The guys looked at one another, taking a moment to absorb that information. "You think he crossed over to the other side. Got involved with supplying rather than attempting to stem the flow of drugs into the US?" Lewis asked.

"He wouldn't be the first one to be tempted. But I gotta say, tough as he seemed to think he was, he would be no match for those coldhearted sons of bitches. If he tried to cross them, or cut them out—"

"Yeah, but if they did order a hit on him, they wouldn't care who was looking into it because they think they're untouchable." Lewis shrugged. "Shit, they probably are."

Hunter nodded. "I see what you mean. They wouldn't know Anais was looking into Gary's disappearance. Even if they did, they wouldn't give a shit."

"Exactly." Hunter rubbed his chin. "So how did the people trying to frighten Anais know she was asking questions?"

"Because Gary wasn't working alone," Lewis replied thoughtfully. "Someone still serving recruited him."

Hunter nodded. "Yeah. Either Gary's still alive, and doesn't want his wife to know it, or the person who got Gary involved doesn't want anyone delving."

"Delving is what we do best." Lewis grinned. "So what are we gonna do to flush them out."

Hunter's expression was grim and determined. "If ever a situation called for a trap, then this is it."

"I agree, but we don't know how they got onto Anais in the first place, so how can we lure them into a trap?"

Hunter answered Lewis's question with one of his own. "How did Raoul get Gary's service record?"

"Ah, of course. Computer hacking."

"Right. I think we're up against a fairly sophisticated and ruthless operation. Besides, like we said the other day, any teen with above average computer knowledge can hack into stuff, especially ordinary e-mail accounts with no special protection."

"You think they hacked Anais's e-mail?"

"Well, she told us that was the method she used to start asking questions."

"Ah, so you're going to suggest she sends out a message saying she has more information about Gary's disappearance." Lewis scowled. "But who would she send the message to, and why?"

"To one of the last people to see him before he disappeared. She could imply that person might know something to help her." Hunter thought of Tony Regan, in his wheelchair, with a grudge to bear against Harrison and an ever-greater need to feel useful. "And I know just the person she can ask."

Chapter Ten

Anais woke early, feeling invigorated, refreshed and enlightened. She sat up and stretched, grinning when she recalled the games she had played with Hunter and Lewis the day before. She was a little sore, but pleasantly so, and more than ready for her next lesson. She had always thought herself to be a woman of the world. Now she realized just how sheltered her life had actually been. *It's never too late to learn.*

With that thought in mind she jumped up and hit the shower. Ten minutes later she went downstairs, following the smell of freshly-brewed coffee and frying bacon, ravenous again, prepared to face whatever the day threw at her, preferably Hunter and Lewis.

Hunter was in the kitchen, cooking breakfast. Lewis sat at the counter, reading the paper.

"Morning, babe," Hunter said without turning around from the stove. "Sleep well?"

How did they do that? She didn't think she had made any sound, but they knew she was there without even having to look up.

"Just fine, thanks."

Hunter chuckled. "I wonder why?"

Lewis put the paper aside and sent her a slow, devastatingly sexy smile, which was all it took to get her juices flowing again. God, but she was pathetic!

"You look good enough to eat." He stood up and pulled her into his arms for a kiss that didn't last nearly long enough for her liking. "Just in time for breakfast, too."

"What are we doing today?" she asked, closing eyes to savor a sinfully delicious bite of eggs Benedict.

"Well, we have news." She opened her eyes again and paid close attention as Hunter told her Gary had been deployed to Honduras on counter-narcotic duties. "He did three tours there, and we think that's where he perfected his Spanish."

"Oh, I see."

"We also think he might have gotten involved in working with the drug traffickers rather than against them," Lewis added.

She put her silverware aside, no longer hungry. "I can't imagine that," she said. "Gary was far from perfect, but he *was* a patriot."

"Did you know he'd been up on charges several times?" Hunter placed a large, comforting hand on her thigh. "He had anger management issues, and there were violent outbursts against other soldiers, problems taking orders, that sort of stuff."

"No, I didn't know." She shook her head. "It seems there's a lot I didn't know about the man I married."

Hunter squeezed the thigh he was still caressing. "It's looking increasingly likely that Gary is still alive."

Anais gasped. "Why do you say that?"

"The military wouldn't have trashed your place, or threatened you. If he was in league with the Hondurans, they wouldn't care if you were trying to find him. They wouldn't even know."

"The only person who would worry about you asking questions would be Gary," Lewis added, "because he either doesn't want to be found, or doesn't want you involved."

Anais's head whirled, and she had trouble absorbing all the information the guys had just hit her with. Not once had it occurred to her that Gary might actually be alive. The question was, how did she feel about it if he was?

"I still find it hard to imagine he would do such a thing," she said weakly, wondering why she sprang so automatically to his defense when she no longer sure what he would do.

"We could be way off base here," Hunter replied. "But you need to bear in mind that he was angry at being disciplined, so probably felt the need to fight back."

"I suppose, but…but how did he know I was asking?"

"We think he hacked into your e-mail, darlin'," Lewis said.

She offered them a wry smile. "There seems to be a lot of hacking going down."

"The thing is," Hunter said. "If he has crossed to the other side, he couldn't have done it without help from a serving solider in a position of authority, someone who could alter records and make sure people were looking the wrong way at the right time. We think that person kept an eye on the military's investigation into Gary's death, learned you were asking questions, and let Gary know."

"How would one man, a part of a squad, be able to divert drugs without anyone noticing?" she asked.

"He wouldn't need to. Drugs are flown out of places like Honduras in light aircraft that operate out of a whole raft of tiny dirt strips, not even proper runways, that are tucked away all over the country. There are so many of them it would be impossible for the US to keep tracks of them all. It's equally easy for them to land in mainland USA without being traced. The irony is that all commercial aircraft are under ever tighter scrutiny, but private airfields are more or less unregulated. All Gary would have to do would be to let his contacts know which areas the troops were targeting on their next raids in Honduras. The military wouldn't be that surprised if the smugglers stayed one step ahead of them. They have contacts everywhere, and everyone knows the so-called war against drugs is a losing battle."

"But I still don't get it. Money has never bothered Gary." Anais sent Hunter a bewildered look. "Why would he turn against his country?"

"If he did," Hunter said softly, his hand still caressing her thigh, "and if he's still alive, I guess that's a question you can ask him yourself."

Anais sat a little straighter, anger replacing her earlier confusion. Hunter and Lewis wouldn't have suggested Gary might still be alive, and a traitor, if they weren't fairly sure of their facts. Anais knew their relationship had been going through a rocky patch, but how could he do this to her? Had he really just taken off and left her hanging? Well, if Gary had and was the one now trying to frighten her, he had a surprise in store. He was about to discover that nowadays Anais was more than just a trusting little wife who stood by her man no matter what.

"Do you think the military suspect?" she asked.

"It would explain why the investigation became *eyes only*," Lewis replied. "And why your Major Dixon got called in. He doesn't do small cases."

"So, how are we going to prove or disprove your theory?"

"By luring him into a trap." Hunter removed his hand from her thigh and slid it around her waist instead. She leaned her head against his shoulder, grateful for its support. "Are you up for that?"

"You'd better believe it."

"Atagirl!" Lewis grinned at her. "I'll let Hunter explain the plan."

"I'm going to ask Tony Regan, the guy with MS and an ax to grind against your husband, to help us out," Hunter said. "You're gonna e-mail him, and ask to meet with him at your apartment."

"Why there? The guy's in a wheelchair. Surely it would be more convenient if I went to him."

"We need you to be in your apartment because of the bug," Hunter replied. "If Gary, or whoever planted it learns of the meeting, he will want to know what goes down. The bug has limited range, so he will have to park close by in order to listen."

"There are only so many places where he can park to get the best reception," Lewis explained. "We'll be there watching, and we'll get the tag number of the guy's car, take pictures of him to see if you recognize him, and go from there."

"You make it all sound so straightforward," Anais said. "What if someone tries to get to us in my apartment?"

Hunter's jaw flexed and hardened. "We won't let that happen."

"I'm not scared for myself, but if Tony Regan is handicapped, it might not go so well for him."

"Don't let Tony hear you say that," Hunter replied.

She fell silent for a moment, assessing the risk, not for her but for Tony. "Okay, if you're sure Tony wants to put himself at risk, I'll do it, too. What do you want me to say in my e-mail?"

"I need to call Tony first, make sure he's good with it," Hunter said. "In the meantime Lewis is gonna go back to your apartment, make sure you haven't had any more visitors in the last couple of days, and check on the range of the bug."

"I'm on it," Lewis said, standing up and reaching for the keys to their truck.

"You go sit on the deck and relax, honey," Hunter said. "I'll go and call Tony, then come and join you."

Anais nodded and drifted outside. It was the time of year when the weather in Florida was just about perfect. Not too hot, not too much humidity, a crystal-clear sky and a light breeze coming off the water, fanning her face. She fell into one of the comfortable loungers and allowed her mind to drift, thinking about all Hunter and Lewis had just told her, wondering if it could actually be true. It sounded plausible, unless you knew Gary Harrison as well as Anais did. He was a fitness fanatic, disinclined to even drink beer. He had never smoked, cared about what he ate, and would run a mile rather than touch drugs. As far as she knew, he wasn't interested in other women, didn't gamble, and had no debts or vices. He was almost too good to be true.

So why would he be tempted into helping drug runners? What could possibly have tempted him? It made absolutely no sense.

Against all the odds and in spite of her differences with Gary, she wanted the guys to be wrong about him, if only because they had once loved one another deeply. Anais didn't want to think she was such a bad judge of character that she could fall in love with a guy capable of bringing poison into the country that was targeted at vulnerable kids. Besides, if Gary had changed sides, surely she would have noticed differences in him. Well, she had, she supposed. He had changed in so far as he'd become more remote, harder to reach, but she'd put that down to operational fatigue. If the signs had been there, she ought to have noticed them.

"All fixed," Hunter said, joining her on the deck and sinking onto the seat beside her. "Tony understands and looks forward to receiving your e-mail."

"Does he fully appreciate that he's putting himself at risk?"

"Sure, but like he says himself, what does he have to lose? He knows his days are numbered. Besides, I think he enjoys the idea of helping you. He has a score to settle with your husband."

"That's so sad, about his condition, I mean. I met him a few times. He's a nice guy."

"He says the same thing about you."

"Well then, we can't both be wrong." Anais forced a smile, when all she really felt was a great deal of tension and an overwhelming desire to get this over with. "Shall we go send the e-mail?"

"Wait until Lewis gets back and gives us the all clear with your apartment."

"Oh, okay."

They fell silent for a while, and Anais, feeling secure with Hunter beside her, and yet oddly restless, reached for his hand. His long, capable fingers closed around her palm and squeezed. His chocolate-brown eyes softened as he looked at her.

"I know this is tough for you, a lot to take in, but it will be okay, darlin'," he said. "We'll soon know one way or another."

"Yes." She sighed. "Talk about something else. Take my mind off things."

"What would you like to talk about?"

"You. Lewis tells me you missed out on college and went into the army straight from high school."

Hunter's expression closed down and, sensing that he seldom spoke about his early years, she wondered if he would answer her. She allowed the silence to stretch between them until, staring off into the distance, Hunter broke it.

"My mom died when I was ten. I was the oldest of four. I have two younger sisters, a brother, and a father who was..." Hunter grimaced, and Anais was glad the concentrated fury in his expression wasn't directed at her. He was, she realized, a dangerous man to cross. When unleashed, the not-quite-civilized aspect of his character—of most military men's characters—would be a lethal weapon in its own right. "My father was a bully and a tyrant. He took his belt to us for the most minor transgressions. Not in the way that I whip your cute butt," he added, the anger leaving his eyes as he caressed her face with the fingers of the hand not holding hers, "but sadistically, with the deliberate intention of causing us serious pain. With every beating my anger increased. I guess I was just waiting for my moment. It came when I was fourteen and I caught him trying to do something other than beat my sister. I was as big as he was by then and a damned sight fitter, with all sorts of pent-up resentments to work out, and I knocked seven shades of shit out of him. When I look back on it, I'm surprised I didn't kill him. Anyway, I threw him out of the house, told him never to come near us again, and he had the good sense to take me seriously. None of us have seen him since. I've no idea if he's alive or dead, and don't give a shit either way."

"Good for you, for throwing him out, I mean." Anais felt tears of sympathy welling. "No wonder you don't want kids of your own, if that's the only parental example you ever had. You must have had a terrible childhood."

"It wasn't the best, but it got better after that. I looked out for my siblings myself, and we turned out okay, all things considered."

"How did you manage that?" she asked, astounded yet impressed. "You were only a kid yourself. What about money? Didn't welfare stick their noses in?"

"I got our grandmother, my mom's mom, to move in and help us. She had wanted to ever since Mom passed, but *he* wouldn't have her anywhere near us. That would have spoiled his fun, you see, because she would have stopped him from bullying us." Hunter scowled at the memory. "Anyway, Gran and I between us raised the others, kept them on the straight and narrow, while I worked two jobs and graduated high school."

"You didn't have a childhood."

"We all deal with the hand life deals us, darlin'." He grinned, appearing to shake off the anger of unpalatable memories, and kissed the top of her head. "Besides, I'm making up for lost time now, a bit like you are."

"But why the military?"

"Because I was in *lurve*," Hunter replied with transparent reluctance.

"At eighteen?"

"Yep. She was just about the prettiest little thing I'd ever seen. She went to the same school as me, was real popular, a cheerleader and all that. I wasn't on the football team. Didn't have time for games. I had to work to support my family, so I didn't imagine she would look twice at me."

"I think you must have underestimated your charisma even then," Anais said, intrigued. "What happened? Presumably it didn't end well."

"No, it didn't." Hunter threw his head back and closed his eyes. "Blame youth and inexperience, but when we started dating, I thought I'd found my soul mate. She was going on to college locally, I was going to get a job in construction. There was a housing boom in

Florida about that time, and I could earn top dollar. We never talked about marriage, but I just kinda assumed. Anyway, we couldn't keep our hands off one another, and when she told me she was pregnant I thought what the heck, she won't be able to go to college, but we were gonna marry anyway."

Anais gasped. "You have a child?" *And didn't think to mention it.*

"No, honey, I don't, but some preppy guy from the football team does."

Anais clasped a hand to her mouth. "She was cheating on you?"

"Yes, and I would never have known if one of her girlfriends hadn't told me. She'd stolen the football player from her friend, and she was out for revenge. When the ball player found out Sandy was knocked up he dropped her like a hot brick, said it couldn't have been his, so she tried to pass it off as mine."

"How could she do that? The more I learn about your past, the easier it is for me to understand why you don't want kids." Anais shook her head, thinking just how badly she had wanted a child, and how disappointed she had been when Gary insisted they wait. Now she might never have the chance. "It's so unfair that people who least want children seem to have them so irresponsibly."

"Have I hit a raw nerve, talking about kids? I know how much you want one, sweetheart?"

"Yes, I'll admit that, but this isn't about me. I want to know what happened."

"Well, when I found out about the other guy, I asked Sandy if it was true. I really didn't believe it could be, seeing as how what we had going on was so good, but she admitted seeing him. She said they didn't actually get it on and that the baby was mine. We did some calculations, or rather I did, and knew it couldn't be. I'd been away for four weeks working on a project in Miami and hadn't seen Sandy because she'd been doing a tour of possible colleagues. It wasn't physically possible for me to have impregnated her."

"She used you."

"Yeah, her folks went crazy. Her dad was all for using his shotgun on me, until he learned the truth, then he turned his attention to the ball player. I'd had enough, spoke to my gran and she suggested signing up. I never knew my granddaddy, but he'd been a soldier and had loved the life. Gran said I was a lot like him and thought I would take to it, too."

"And you did." Anais leaned forward and brushed her lips against his. "Thanks for telling me. I get the impression you don't often talk about it."

"I *never* talk about it. The past is the past. But you're easy to talk to, and besides, I wanted you to know."

"No wonder you never married, after having a father like yours and then having the woman you thought you loved trying to dupe you."

Hunter cocked a brow. "I do have issues with trust, I guess. A shrink would have a field day with all the stuff going on inside my head."

"You had a childhood from hell, and yet Lewis's was ideal." She shrugged. "They say opposites attract."

"Is that what he told you? That his childhood was all peachy?"

"Well, yes, in not so many words."

Hunter laughed. "Lewis can be economical with the truth sometimes. His family was close knit, but also fiercely competitive. His father's a corporate lawyer, and Lewis was expected to follow in his footsteps, regardless of what he wanted for himself. When he decided to join up they disowned him, and not one of them has spoken to him since."

Anais gasped. "But that's awful. If they loved him, surely they wanted him to be happy?"

"Yeah, just so long as his version of happiness coincided with theirs."

"Lewis said he was picked on a lot for being puny."

Hunter laughed. "Hard to credit, ain't it? He experienced first hand how cruel kids can be, and never got any parental help with that. It's one of the reasons he's not too keen to have kids of his own."

"I understand, and he's certainly not lacking in muscle now."

"He saved my ass when we were on assignment once. Saw a sniper's rifle before I did and took the guy out. We wouldn't be sitting here now if it weren't for Lewis. I owe him everything, but don't you dare tell him I told you so. He will be unbearable."

Anais laughed. "Your secret's safe with me."

"Perhaps now you understand why we live, work, and play together."

"Yes I do, and thanks for sharing." She paused. "How are your sisters and brother now?"

"All married with families of their own, and doing a damned sight better job of raising them than the example that was set by our old man."

"From what you've told me, that can't be difficult."

"You got that right."

Still holding hands, they lapsed into a companionable silence. She thought about all Hunter had just told her, wondering if his penchant for chastising his subs was a product of his violent childhood, or whether he did it to prove it could be a controlled, pleasurable, nonaggressive experience. Then again, perhaps he did it just to prove he wasn't his father's son. Anais's heart went out to him. He'd had a tough time of it, been let down by everyone who mattered to him, with the exception of Lewis and his grandmother. No wonder the two guys were so tight.

Anais was warmed by a hot sun and the even hotter male sitting with his thigh jammed up against hers. The sexual magnetism flowed between them like an electric current, filling her senses with an urgent desire.

"Don't even think about it," he said, a smile in his voice.

"About what?"

"About fucking."

"How did you know I—"

"Honey, I can read you like a book. Your eyes go all dark and swirly—"

"My eyes are closed."

"I have X-ray vision. Besides, you also bite your lip, and…" He glanced down at her torso and chuckled. "Your nipples pucker."

She opened her eyes and returned the favor by fixing her gaze on the bulge in his pants. "And you're completely immune to temptation, I suppose?"

"Nope, I'm harder than a loan shark, but we have other things to think about right now. Like setting up this sting to catch your husband. Or not."

"He isn't my husband. The man I married wouldn't just walk out without leaving an explanation. Even if he is still alive, I don't want anything more to do with him."

"I'm glad to hear it, but that's not the point."

"Then what is the point, Mr. Control Freak? We have time on our hands, and I'd rather like you to fuck me, if it's not too much trouble. Where's the harm in that?"

He shook his head, his expression changing from fiercely determined to unsure. "We were rough with you yesterday. You need some recovery time."

"Isn't that up to me to decide?" She wound her arms around his neck, slid onto his lap and tangled her fingers in his ponytail. "I can feel you want to."

He laughed. "You're insatiable."

"And whose fault is that? You're the one that awoke the beast inside of me."

"Hey, look." Hunter pointed to the water. "Dolphins."

"Wow, they're so close."

They watched for a while as a dozen dolphins' heads appeared above the water. Some of them did barrel rolls, others appeared to chase one another. Anais was enchanted.

"They're hunting. Wanna join them?"

"Can we?" Anais asked.

"Sure. Why not?"

He took her hand and led her to the dock. Without seeming to care that they might be seen, he stripped off his jeans and T-shirt. He was naked beneath. Anais took herself down to her pretty underwear but wasn't quite so brave as Hunter and left it in place. He shot her a look, quirked a brow, and laughed.

"Coward."

He took her hand and, knees bent up to their chests, they jumped into the cold water from the end of the dock. Surfacing together, they were really close to the dolphins, who stopped to investigate them. Hunter swam toward them with a strong crawl. Anais followed more slowly, enchanted when a dolphin allowed her to touch its nose. Then it swam off after the rest of the pod.

"That was amazing," Anais said, treading water as she watched it go.

"Yeah, they're pretty curious."

She followed Hunter when he swam back toward the dock. Instead of climbing the ladder, he turned and pulled her into his arms. He could touch the bottom, but the water was too deep for her and she put her arms around his neck to stay afloat. Somehow her legs just happened to work their way around his waist.

"You ever fucked in water before?" he asked.

"Only in the bath with Lewis." She canted her head and smiled at him. "I thought you didn't want to fuck."

"Well, you seem kinda anxious about…everything."

"Oh, so I'm to blame for this?" She bumped her buttocks against his groin.

"Honey, you have no idea."

"Hunter, I'd really love to, but there are houses all along here. We could be seen."

"Only the bits of us that aren't below water," he replied, grinning. "What's the matter? Gone off the idea."

Recklessly, Anais pulled out the band that held his hair in a ponytail, and dug her fingers into his wet locks. With a groan he claimed her lips at the same time as he pulled her sodden panties aside and drove his cock into her. Hard and demanding, just like always. Just like the way she was staring to enjoy it.

"That what you need, baby?" he asked, breaking the kiss.

"Yes, Sir. It feels so damned good."

She moaned when he pulled out again almost immediately.

"Turn around, and hold on to that fender," he said, indicating the floating buoy tied to the dock.

As soon as she did so, Hunter slapped her butt hard beneath the water. "Bad girl," he said. "Bad, bad girl."

And then he was inside her again, from behind, giving it to her hard and urgently. Anais pushed back against him, feeling her orgasm blossoming, just as something loud splashed beside them.

"What am I missing?" Lewis asked, surfacing and pushing the wet hair out of his eyes.

"Our sub was getting antsy," Hunter replied. "Needed to teach her a few manners."

"Quaint teaching method you've got there, buddy."

Hunter laughed. "It's the only one she understands."

"You need some help with her?"

"I'd appreciate it. She's too demanding for me to handle her alone."

Lewis dove again and surfaced below the dock, directly in front of Anais. He attacked her tits with his teeth, while Hunter continued to fuck her from behind. She felt his laden balls slap against her buttocks, and glanced up at all the windows fronting the waterway, wondering if they were being watched. No longer embarrassed at the prospect, the thought was now a real turn-on. She would never last two minutes like this. No one had forbidden her to come, so she buried the fingers of one hand hard into Lewis's shoulders and screamed as she took what she needed from Hunter. She clung to his cock just as tightly as she was holding the buoy with her other hand, floating without any help from the water.

Anais was pleased when Hunter swelled inside her and exploded almost immediately after she finished coming. Mr. Self-Control wasn't quite so controlled as he would have her believe.

The realization was empowering.

Chapter Eleven

Once they were all showered and dressed again, Hunter got right down to business, pleased to see that Anais looked calmer, and more in control. He really hadn't meant to fuck her in the water like that, had he? The dolphins were just supposed to be a distraction—a way to mark time until Lewis returned. Yeah, right, keep telling yourself that.

He still didn't quite know why he'd given her chapter and verse on his childhood. He didn't talk about those days. There never seemed to be any point. It would never change, which is why he had avoided shrinks. He didn't need some overpaid naval gazer to tell him he had hang-ups about his youth, and the bitch who'd tried to foist her child off on him. In his darkest moments he was still haunted by his father's bitter, angry face, and yet talking to Anais about him had somehow put the nightmare into perspective. His old man could no longer hurt him.

"How was Anais's apartment?" he asked Lewis as they took coffee together in the lounge.

"As I left it. No one's been in, and the bug's still in place."

"How can you be sure no one's been there?" Anais asked.

"We have our ways," Lewis replied, waggling his brows at her.

"Oh okay, play James Bond if it makes you feel good."

Lewis blew her a kiss. "You make me feel good, darlin'."

"Did you figure out where anyone might watch the place from if they want to listen in?" Hunter asked.

"Yeah, there are only two places, but the most likely is in a bar's parking lot immediately opposite. It's close enough for good reception, and a strange car parked there wouldn't be out of place. The only other spot is within the grounds of the apartment block. There's no gateman, nothing to stop strangers driving in, but there is a super who might notice someone sitting in a car that doesn't belong to a resident."

"So you think the bar's lot is the more likely place?"

Lewis nodded. "It's where I'd sit, and it's easy to make a quick getaway if necessary."

"Then we'll watch both locations but concentrate on the bar's lot." Hunter smiled at Anais. "Okay, darlin', it's time to send the e-mail to Tony."

"I need to have a reason not to have been at home since the place was vandalized. If they're watching they will know I haven't been there."

"Good point." Hunter nodded. "I don't think they're watching all the time. That visit was strictly a one-off, but you're right to say we need to cover all bases. Do you have a reason to go away? One that would sound right to Gary if he heard it."

"I sometimes have to go to the headquarters of the publishers I edit for. We have editorial meetings, pitch for books we want to acquire, stuff like that."

"That would work." Hunter paced the room, thinking aloud. "You'll tell Tony that the super noticed your broken door and called you on your cell about it. You asked him to get it fixed, which he did. He noticed your computer missing, but nothing else seemed to be, so you told him not to file a report to the police."

"Hang on, if she's on her way back from the publishing meeting, why didn't she have her laptop with her?"

"I have an iPad I travel with," Anais replied to Lewis's question.

"Then we'll make sure your e-mail to Tony goes from your iPad, which I assume is in your purse."

"Right."

"We'll send him a picture of the writing on the bathroom mirror as well. You'll tell Tony you're freaked out about it, but want answers more urgently than ever. You have a few new theories about Gary's disappearance you want to run past him in person. You'll be home later this afternoon. Would he mind coming over? He did offer to help you the last time you spoke by e-mail, which is true."

They spent some time getting the wording of the e-mail exactly right.

"Are we happy with that?" Anais and Lewis nodded in response to Hunter's question. "Then press send."

"There, it's gone," Anais said.

"Right, we'll have some lunch, then you need to drive back in your own car, babe," Hunter said. "We'll be right behind you."

"I'm not sure I can eat much. I'm pretty nervous."

"If you don't want to do this, we'll think of another way," Lewis said, touching her hand.

"No, I definitely want to do it. I guess I'm just a bit scared about what I might find out, but I do really need to know."

"I guess you do," Hunter replied.

She grinned. "If Gary *is* alive, he won't remain that way for long once I get my hands on the lying jerk."

The guys both laughed. "Atagirl!"

Hunter made tuna sandwiches for lunch, after which it was time to leave. He and Lewis helped Anais into the driving seat of her car and closed the door once she was inside. She opened the window, but the smile she sent them didn't reach her eyes.

"Wish me luck," he said.

"You don't need to worry, darlin'." Hunter reached out and touched her face. "No one will try to get to you this afternoon, but I'll bet my bank balance they'll be there to listen, just to make sure you don't know anything. Are you sure you know what to say?"

"Yes, we've been over it a dozen times."

"If it helps, imagine Gary being in the room with you, listening to every word. Think before you speak. Don't say anything you wouldn't want him to hear, but try to come across naturally at the same time."

Anais grimaced. "No pressure then."

"You can do it." Hunter leaned through the window and stole a kiss. "I have every faith in you."

"Thanks, but I need to go now, before I lose my nerve."

She wound the window up and drove out of the garage. The guys jumped into their truck and were right behind her. They watched her drive into her block, and stop to have a few words with the super, just like they'd told her to. If she really was returning from a trip then she would want to speak to him about the break in. She then grabbed an overnight bag Hunter had supplied her with from her trunk and headed to her apartment.

"She must be scared silly, but you'd never know it," Lewis said admiringly.

"Yep." Hunter killed the engine and jumped out of the truck, followed by Lewis. "Right, buddy, you get the better job. Go sit at the bar opposite, drink a beer and keep a careful watch on the lot."

"Will do," Lewis replied, grabbing a newspaper from the truck that was folded open to the sports section.

"I'll be around the back, watching the only other possible place. I'll also see if anyone goes near her condo."

"Text if you need me. I'll do the same."

Hunter slapped Lewis's shoulder. "Right, let's do it."

* * * *

Anais's hands were shaking so badly that it took her three attempts to turn the key in her new lock. When she finally managed to push the door open, she half expected someone to jump out from behind the furniture. She told herself to get a grip. Lewis had been here just this morning and checked the place out. Everything was fine. It smelled a little musty. It also smelled of cleaning fluid. Someone, Lewis presumably, had eradicated all signs of the break-in, for which she was grateful. She opened the drapes and then the doors to the terrace, allowing sunlight to pour into her living space and wipe out some of her anxiety. Bogeymen don't hide in broad daylight.

She walked through the apartment, satisfying herself everything was where it should be, more or less. She had loved this light, airy apartment the first time she saw it, and knew she had to buy it. Now it had been violated, her personal space invaded. She would never feel comfortable in it again, and would probably sell.

She gasped when she entered the bathroom. The mirror had been scrubbed clean, but she could still see a feint outline of the words that had been scrawled across it. Refusing to allow it to get to her, she wandered back into the living room and made some iced tea. It would be another half hour at least before Tony arrived, and time hung heavily on her hands. She remembered what the guys had told her to do, and flipped on the radio, just so there was some noise and anyone listening would know she was home.

She took her iced tea out to the terrace and tried to remain calm. Patience had never been her strong point, but she was rewarded when the door bell sounded ten minutes ahead of time. She peered through the spy-hole, just to make sure it was Tony. She panicked when she couldn't see anyone.

"Look lower," said a voice.

Of course, Tony would be in his wheelchair. Embarrassed yet reassured, she opened the door and tried not to show her shock at the deterioration in the vibrant man she remembered seeing not so long ago at a social function at the base.

"Hey, Tony, come in. Thanks so much for coming. Can you manage?"

"Sure, I've had plenty of time to practice driving this thing." He adroitly maneuvered his chair into the room and Anais closed the door. "You have good wheelchair access to this building, too, which helps. Not all the older blocks do."

Anais switched the radio off, not wanting it to drown out their conversation. "I'm so sorry to see you like this," she said, deciding not to pussyfoot around the subject of his disability in the way people often did. Besides, it was true, and she wanted him to hear it. "You don't deserve it."

"Thanks, but don't let it bother you." He grinned. "I try not to. Not everyone gets advance warning of how long they have left. It kinda makes you concentrate on the important stuff."

"I can imagine." But Anais couldn't, not really, and his attitude put her own problems firmly into perspective. She wondered if she would be able to look at the world so prosaically if she were in his position, and was humbled by his attitude. "I was just having some iced tea. Can I get you a glass?"

"Yeah, that would be good."

"Shall we take it outside?" Tony frowned at her, and she realized her mistake. They were supposed to remain inside so the bug picked up their conversation. Jeez, she was *so* not good at all this cloak and dagger stuff. "Or is to too warm for you?"

"I'm better in here, thanks. I don't do well in direct sunlight."

"Of course, I'm sorry."

Tony moved his chair so he was facing her seat, and then winked at her. "I was sorry about Gary," he said. "I won't pretend we were buddies, far from it, but it can't have been easy for you. Now you tell me this place was broken into and you were warned off from trying to find out what happened to him."

"Exactly, but I don't frighten so easily. Besides, I can't move on with my life until I know what happened to him. I don't believe Gary was taken by a 'gator, as the military would have me believe. Do you?"

"Frankly, no. I didn't like the guy, but I'd be the first to admit he had probably forgotten more about survival than I'll ever know. He had a great respect for the big outdoors and would never make that sort of basic mistake."

"That's what I think. And I've...err, found out he did three consecutive tours to Honduras on counter-narcotic assignments."

"Really?" Tony winked again, but sounded convincingly surprised. "How did you get to learn that? It's classified."

"I still have a few friends in high places who don't like to see me being stonewalled."

"Obviously." Tony paused. "You're wondering if he made enemies over there, and they took him out?"

"The thought crossed my mind. It's certainly one explanation."

"How did you think I could help? I've never been deployed to Honduras."

"It's a long shot, but you worked with him several times when he was reassigned to training. I wondered, after what I've just told you, if anything he said could cast light on what happened to him?"

"I can't think of a single thing. Sorry, Anais, I'd like to help, but I spent as much time as I could avoiding Gary."

"Do you know anyone who might have been deployed with him? Perhaps they could help."

"I can ask, but I don't hold out much hope. If they're still serving, they can't say much. If they got out, the chances are they're scattered far and wide, and still wouldn't talk anyway."

"Oh well, it was just a thought." Anais shook her head, no longer acting. "It's so damned frustrating, not knowing."

"My advice is to let it go and get on with your life. There's no profit in dwelling on the past."

"No, I guess not, and I would do that, but for the break-in here. Something isn't right. I mean, in my place, wouldn't you be curious?"

"Sure, but—"

"Gary and I were childhood sweethearts. He wasn't always as hard as the army made him become. We had our differences recently, but I still need to know what happened to him."

"I understand. Okay, leave it with me and I'll ask around."

"Thanks so much." Tony wheeled his chair toward the door, and Anais walked along beside him. "I really appreciate it."

"No problem. You just lock your door and stay safe now."

"I need to go to the store. I have no food in. Once I've done that, I shall follow your advice."

Anais closed the door after Tony, and leaned against it, emotionally exhausted after her little performance. She waited five minutes until her cell phone vibrated with a text message from Hunter, telling her the coast was clear. She lost no time in leaving her apartment and jumping in her car to drive back to the guys' place. She wasn't surprised when a navy blue truck fell right in behind her.

"You should be an actress," Hunter said, helping her from her car and giving her a hug.

"Did I do okay?"

"You fooled me," Lewis replied.

The three of them moved into the living room. "Did you see anyone watching?" Anais asked.

"Lewis did, in the bar's parking lot. A black truck with tinted windows and a whole heap of large antennae. It pulled in just after he got there and stayed until Tony left your apartment. The guy driving didn't get out, and so we couldn't get a picture of him, but we did get his tag."

"Can you find out who the truck's registered to?"

Hunter laughed. "I'll try not to take that as an insult."

"Sorry, I guess I'm still a bit on edge."

"Just give me a moment. I'll give Raoul a call and he'll run it down for me."

"Okay. Was it a Florida tag?"

"Yeah, it was."

Lewis poured Anais a glass of wine, which she nervously sipped at while Hunter made his call. He returned a short time later, brandishing a piece of paper.

"Does the name Taylor Sanchez mean anything to you, babe?" he asked.

"Taylor was Gary's father's name," she said slowly, "but Sanchez means nothing."

"It's a Spanish connection, though," Lewis said.

"An odd sort of name," Hunter mused. "Taylor isn't Spanish. It sounds kinda made up. Raoul is doing a check on the guy, but I don't figure it will lead far."

"Where does he live?" Lewis asked.

"Not that far." Hunter pulled up Google Earth on his laptop and put in an address in Immokalee, Collier County. "An easy distance if you want to keep tabs on your old job and your former wife."

"If Gary's still alive, surely he'd relocate a long way away?" Anais said.

"Not necessarily." Hunter looked up, offering her a gentle smile. "People gravitate toward the familiar. Immokalee is sparsely populated, former Indian country, close to the 'Glades. Properties are tucked away all over the place. It's easy to hide out, not talk to anyone, and see if anyone's onto you before they get too close."

"Hiding in plain sight?" she suggested.

"Right."

"Sounds like Gary's sort of place," Lewis remarked, pointing to the close up of the property on the screen. "Plenty of private land to keep him isolated, and close to nature so he can do all the stuff he does best."

"I still don't get it." Anais shook her head. "What the heck is going on?"

Hunter grinned at her. "Only one way to find out. How do you fancy a trip to Immokalee?"

Chapter Twelve

"When do we leave?" Anais asked.

Hunter laughed. "Is tomorrow soon enough for you?"

"I guess I can wait that long." She followed Hunter into the kitchen. "Let me help you with dinner."

"No, I've got it covered. You just take it easy."

Anais was too keyed up to simply kick her heels. If she didn't have an occupation she would brood, and her imagination would get away from her. Hardly surprising, given that her fink of a husband had probably faked his own death. Hadn't he heard of divorce, for fuck's sake? Sighing, she grabbed her laptop from the study and settled on the settee with it. She was getting behind with her editing so made an effort to lose herself in the work she loved. Lewis was working on his laptop, too, but he'd brought it into the sitting room, as though he didn't want to leave her alone. Hunter puttered about in the kitchen with his usual tight efficiency, but kept throwing her reassuring smiles. Anais cherished the domesticity because she had never had it with Gary, and hadn't realized she needed it.

"I was right about Sanchez," Hunter said over dinner. "I just heard back from Raoul. It's a stolen identity. There's nothing goes back more than a couple of years."

"I see."

"We managed to get the picture from his driving license," Lewis added.

"Is it him?" she asked anxiously.

"Hard to say," Hunter replied.

"Show me."

"Come on then." He stood up and held out his hand. "If you're done here, the picture's on my computer in the study."

The three of them crossed the hall and Hunter pulled up the picture in question. Anais steeled herself to take a look. Now that the moment of truth had arrived, she was unsure if she wanted to know. She closed her eyes for an expressive moment and took a deep breath. Then she opened them again and looked at the screen. The man in the picture had long dark hair, a heavy beard and dull green eyes.

"Gary had a buzz cut, was clean shaven, and had gray eyes," she said slowly. "But it's him. I recognize his nose and the shape of his jaw, even through that beard." She exhaled sharply, endeavoring not to hyperventilate. "He's alive."

Hunter slid an arm around her shoulders and pulled her against him. "Take a moment, babe. You've had a shock."

"No, I'm okay. You got me used to the idea, so it's not that much of a surprise. I'm not upset, I'm just plain mad."

"Mad is good," Lewis replied. "Mad helps a lot in these situations."

"We can do one of two things." Hunter moved to the love seat they had recently…well, made love on, and took Anais with him. He sat down with her. Lewis perched a buttock on the small amount of remaining space on her opposite side. She felt crowded by them, but in a good way. Protected, cared about, cherished—feelings she hadn't known for a long time, if ever. "We can either go to Immokalee ourselves tomorrow and check out the situation, or tell the military what we've found out and let them deal with it. It's your call, babe."

"Not a chance! The military have cut me out every step of the way. I want to face the lying son of a bitch and see what he has to say for himself. Then we'll call in the military police and have them arrest his sorry ass."

"See," Lewis said, leaning in for a kiss. "I told you mad was good."

"Just so long as you're sure," Hunter said. "It's obvious he doesn't want to be found, and that he's into something heavy. It could get dangerous."

"Yeah, I might rip his head from his shoulders," Anais replied, quietly seething through her hurt and bewilderment. "So he's the one in danger."

"Come on, darlin'," Hunter said. "You need a distraction, and I know just the thing."

"You won't be needing clothes for what we have in mind," Lewis added. "Take them all off right now."

Anais was feeling so overloaded emotionally, that she couldn't have imagined thinking about anything other than Gary's cruel deception. The moment Hunter spoke in his Dom voice and Lewis ordered her to strip, she found out just how wrong she had been. Thoughts of Gary fled her mind at warp speed, replaced by feelings of excitement and anticipation. The guys had already taught her so much, but she got the impression things were about to heat up even more, if that was possible. *Bring it on!*

She shed her clothes and adopted a submissive pose, waiting to be told what to do next.

"Come with us."

Each guy took one of her hands and led her down the stairs. Oh good, they must be going to the playroom. She rather liked their playroom, and all the fascinating toys they had in it. She had no idea what half of them were for, but was very anxious to experiment. Her anger gave way to excitement as she padded naked down the stairs. She wondered who this person was, casually parading about in the buff in front of not one but two relative strangers.

She thought of Gary's callous behavior and realized this was who she was supposed to be. All her life up to this point had been marking time. Hunter and Lewis had believed in her, had brought her alive and awoken her sexuality. That was cause for celebration, not embarrassment, especially since she had fallen violently in love with them both. She almost stumbled when that thought struck home. Hunter's strong arm snaked out and steadied her.

"Careful," he said, his brown eyes softening as he looked down at her. "We need you in one piece."

Was it really possible to fall in love in just two days?

Evidently so. Not that she would ever admit to her feelings. Neither of them was in the market for love, they had made that abundantly clear, and she wasn't about to repay their kindness by making them feel awkward. No, she would just take what was on offer for as long as they were prepared to offer it, and then move on without making a fuss.

Yes, that was definitely what she would do.

"Okay, sweet thing," Hunter said when they were inside the playroom. "I think you're ready for a real high experience."

He pointed to a contraption she hadn't seen before. It looked as though it wouldn't be out of place in a gym. "This is our version of a stockade, complete with impalers and just about every other toy imaginable. Wanna give it a go?"

"Yes, Master Hunter. It sounds like fun."

"Get down on your hands and knees."

Anais felt her juices trickling down her thighs as she got into position. Both the guys had removed their shirts but kept their pants on. Massive bulges tented the areas surrounding their zippers.

"This is our one-stop bondage station," Lewis explained, "complete with mechanical fucker."

With what?

They helped her climb between the various poles. She found there was a comfortable rest for her chest, and her tits fell free on either side of it. She felt shackles being placed around her ankles and wrists and a collar was put around her neck, with light-weight chains attached to it. Clamps on the ends of those chains were placed on her nipples. If she moved her head, even fractionally, harsh pressure was put on her nipples. Before she could get used to that sensation, slick fingers played with her backside. Hunter's, if she had to guess. He seemed obsessed with her ass, and after all the amazing things he'd done with it recently, who was she to complain? Without telling her to expect it, something harder than his fingers slid into it.

"The fucker," Hunter explained. "Turn sideways, honey, and look in the mirror."

She did so and gasped. Was that wild woman, all chained up, taking a vibrator up her backside, and severe pressure on her nipples, really her? The guys had shed their pants now and were sporting impressive erections as they watched her watching herself.

"You have limited movement there, Anais," Hunter explained, like she hadn't already figured that out for herself. "Just keep real still while I punish you and you'll do just fine. This is a mop flogger." He tapped a multi-thronged implement against his hand. "It has wide soft leather strips that give a pleasant sensation, like a massage. Would you like me to chastise you with it?"

"Yes, Master Hunter," she said, panting with need, feeling sexier than ever before, and totally in tune with her two gorgeous tormentors. "If it would please you."

"Pleasure and pain, baby," he said, bringing the flogger down hard over her ass without removing the fucker. "Gotta love those endorphins when they start flowing."

He continued to flay her ass, while Lewis slid beneath her and nipped at her pussy. The sensation drove her crazy, making it impossible to keep still. The moment she tried to move, the collar cut into her airways, causing her to choke.

"Move again and I'll bolt the fucker in place," Hunter warned. "Then you won't be able to move a muscle."

"Sorry, Sir. I'll try not to move, but it's hard."

"We're hard for you, sweetheart, and we'll give you what you need when we're ready, not a moment sooner."

"The more you disobey us," Lewis added, "the longer we'll make you wait."

She wanted to tell them that was just plain mean, but wasn't prepared to risk them backing off. She wouldn't put it past them. Their control appeared to be absolute, while she was literally falling apart because she wanted them so bad.

Every muscle in Anais's body burned with the need to move. She could actually smell the genital scent of their arousal, could see their massive cocks twitching in anticipation in the periphery of her vision, and understood this was a test of obedience. They wouldn't really hurt her, would they? No, she was being foolish. Of course they wouldn't. She heard them moving again and glanced in the mirror. Both of them were standing to one side, staring down at her, grasping their cocks in their hands and working them like they planned to ejaculate over her. *No, not over me. Come inside me, please!* She dared not say the words aloud, but willed them to hear her thoughts. She was on the verge of safe wording them because she couldn't hold this position for a second longer when Hunter appeared to notice the trembling in her limbs.

Without saying a word, he and Lewis released her and helped her to her feet. Blood flowed into her cramped limbs as feeling gradually returned to them. Hunter swept her from the floor, tossed her over his shoulder and paddled her ass with the flat of his hand. He threw her into what appeared to be a wide leather swing suspended just above the floor, and crawled into it with her. It swayed, and she thought at first they might topple out of it, but the motion slowed and they were fine. They hadn't removed the collar from her neck, and Lewis reached up to fasten it to the top of the swing, anchoring her in place but leaving a little bit of play on the chain, and her limbs free.

"On your side," Hunter said curtly.

She swiveled in position, careful not to put any pressure on her neck. She felt Lewis climb up behind her. Surely this contraption wasn't strong enough to take all three of them? There was no ominous creaking, and so Anais slowly relaxed, enjoying herself now as the hammock swayed gently beneath their combined weight. Lewis's hands rubbed patterns on her shoulders, while Hunter's tongue slowly worked its way across her aching tits.

"Did you know," Lewis said, "that frequent orgasms increase the level of the hormone oxytocin? You need oxytocin, so we're doing you a favor by fucking you. It's linked to personality, passion, social skills and a whole bunch of other emotions that are beneficial for sexual health as well as empowering brain function."

"No, Master Lewis, I didn't know that, but I like to be healthy so it sounds like a good reason to have lots of orgasms."

Hunter, in the process of teasing a nipple between his teeth, choked on a laugh and almost bit it off. Wild sensation sizzled through Anais's bloodstream at the harsh contact. Lewis chuckled as his hands progressed south to her backside, and played with her anus. She didn't hesitate to let his fingers penetrate her. After that object Hunter had just used, they felt almost soft and nonintrusive.

Almost.

"That's it, baby," he said in a soft, hypnotic voice. "You're really getting turned on by this, aren't you?"

"Yes, Master Lewis. I like to please you."

"Enough to let us fuck you at the same time?"

* * * *

Lewis held his breath as he waited for her to answer. They probably weren't being fair to her, and should have asked her before they got her so turned on that she would agree to just about anything. They were taking her too far, too fast. They had brought her in here to distract her from thoughts of her jerk of a husband, and hadn't intended to go down this road. But somehow, when they were with Anais, the usual rules of engagement went out the window. She was so frigging hot, so responsive and yet also so vulnerable, that they both had trouble holding themselves back.

He hadn't talked to Hunter about it yet, but Lewis already knew Anais was more than just a sub-in-training. She was special in oh-so-many ways, and Lewis was falling for her. Unless he missed his guess so, too, was Hunter, although with his history he would have a harder time admitting it. His buddy had told him when they drove over to Anais's apartment earlier that he'd spoken to her about his childhood, and about Sandy. Now that had surprised Lewis. Hunter never talked about his troubled past, even though Lewis had always thought it was a bad thing to keep all that negativity bottled up. Seems like the empathy of a good woman—the right woman—was all it had taken for Hunter to see the light.

Right woman or not, they now knew her husband was still alive, and Anais had a hell of a lot to deal with. All they could do to help her right now was to take her out of herself with the sex games she found as exciting as he and Hunter did. Lewis was more than happy to oblige.

"Yes," she said breathlessly. "I'm yours to do whatever you wish to with, Masters."

Shit, she's killing me!

"Okay, darlin'." Hunter released the tit he'd been tormenting and grinned at her. "Just keep absolutely still and let us do the work. That collar will make sure you can't move too much, but I know what you're like when you get really turned on, and I don't want you hurting yourself."

"You need to engage all your senses, sweetheart," Lewis said in a deep, deliberately provocative tone. "Breath real slow and deep, close your eyes, and let the sensations find their own level."

He added another finger to the two already exploring her backside, and moved them around. At the same time he bit down on her shoulder blade, then pushed her hair aside and nibbled her neck below the collar, working his way up to the sensitive area behind her ear. She groaned, presumably because Hunter had slipped his length into her tight cunt.

"That's it, babe," Hunter said, his voice rough and raw. "You've got my cock deep inside you now. Get used to it, then you're gonna have Lewis's filling your sweet ass, too."

She mumbled something incoherent and tried to move. Hunter administered a sharp rap to her thigh. Lewis gave her ass the same treatment, then removed his fingers and replaced them with the tip of his cock. Fuck, it was a tight fit!

"That's it, honey, you've got us both now."

Lewis kissed her ear and slid a little deeper. Hunter withdrew almost all the way, making space for him. Then they reversed the process, just as they had many times before. Except it had never mattered more in the past that they give pleasure. They set up a slick tempo, giving her body the treatment it deserved, bringing her alive, making her cry out with a series of needy little moans.

"That's it, baby." Lewis lowered his head and sent a trail of damp kisses down her spinal column. "You can't get enough of our cocks, can you?"

"No, Master Lewis. I really need you both."

She tried to toss her head, and almost choked.

"Keep still!" Hunter administered another sharp rap to her thigh. "We'll punish you if you try to move again."

"Sorry, Master Hunter, but I'm on fire with need and the feelings are too overpowering for me to remain passive."

"I can tell that by the way you're closing around my cock, darlin', but you've gotta learn to be patient."

A low, animalistic protest slipped past her lips. Her keening was deeply, intoxicatingly sensual, reflecting her deep desire for them. Helpless against the raging force of his need, Lewis nodded to Hunter and they upped the tempo. She cried out, and Lewis felt her body tremble and fragment. They both worked her harder until the trembles subsided, then Hunter administered another of his sharp slaps by way of reprimand.

"There will be consequences," he said sternly, not losing his rhythm as their cocks took it in turn to penetrate her body. "No one gave you permission to orgasm."

"Sorry, Master Hunter." Her breath came in shorter and shorter gasps. "Punish me in whatever way you see fit."

A deep, throaty chuckle echoed through Hunter's body. "Count on it."

Lewis played with the soft spongy area just above her backside whenever he withdrew, knowing it would drive her increasingly wild because it was such a sensitive spot. He wanted her to come for a second time before he and Hunter let rip, and sensed it wouldn't take much to tip her over the edge again. She appeared to be deliberately tugging back on the collar, experimenting with auto-asphyxiation. Lewis wasn't surprised. She had an uncanny knack for running before she could walk.

Hunter nodded, and they really worked a number on her.

"You feel that?" Hunter asked her. "My cock is so fucking big, 'cause it's what you do to me, darlin'."

"Yes, I feel it. You're stretching me so wide."

"What about this?" Lewis sank into her, being careful not to penetrate her ass too hard or too deeply. It was a delicate balance, and he needed to ensure that his increasingly frantic desire didn't overcome caution. "You like what I'm doing to your sweet ass, honey?"

"Yes, I love you both, I…shit, guys, I can't hold it."

Her body was in tremble mode again. She screwed up her eyes and this time, Lewis was sure, pulled her neck against the collar quite deliberately. She gasped, panting and bucking her body between them as she went into sensual meltdown. Watching her was too much for Lewis. He couldn't control his need for another second, and gave up the fight to hold back.

"Fuck it, I'm coming too!"

He grabbed her hips and let go, filling her backside with an endless stream of hot sperm. Hunter swore and Lewis sensed him doing the exact same thing at precisely the same time.

When Lewis finally stopped coming and withdrew from her, his first coherent thought was to wonder where their relationship would go after confronting her husband the following day. One thing Lewis knew for absolute sure was that he wouldn't let her go back to the jerk, even if said jerk suggested it. He was even more determined that she wouldn't escape from him and Hunter. He was pretty sure his buddy felt the same way about her, but whether or not he was ready to trust was another matter. Lewis needed to find a way to persuade him, because the three of them made a perfect team.

Lewis had just discovered that trust came easily now that he had found a woman worthy of his trust.

Chapter Thirteen

Hunter carried Anais back upstairs, through his bedroom, and into his shower. Lewis followed right along and the two of them washed every inch of her. When she was dry, she was barely able to keep her eyes open, and stifled a yawn with the back of her hand.

"Come on, sweetheart, let's get you to bed."

"Hmm, not tired." She wrapped her arms around his neck, smiling like a cat who had overdosed on a whole vat of cream. "Want to play some more."

Hunter laughed. "Not a chance."

Lewis flexed a brow, but otherwise made no comment when Hunter pulled back the covers on his oversized bed and placed her right in the middle of it. Sure, he'd surprised Lewis by having her share his bed. Hell, he'd surprised himself. But Anais was vulnerable right now, given what she'd just discovered about her husband. She had also just taken both their cocks at the same time when she was barely used to anal sex, or any sex at all other than vanilla or the self-administered variety. Her courage and feisty curiosity blew Hunter's mind, to say nothing of his heart, and he wasn't prepared to let her out of his sight right now. But only for now. He knew what Anais wanted out of life, marriage, kids especially, the whole nine yards of domestic bliss, and he was afraid to go there.

"Hmm, this is nice," Anais mumbled sleepily as Hunter climbed into bed on one side of her, Lewis the other.

She rested her head on Hunter's chest, Lewis threw a protective arm across her midriff, and she was asleep in seconds. He was conscious of Lewis's quizzical gaze, but ignored it. They couldn't talk without disturbing Anais. Besides, he wasn't sure what there was to say, because he hadn't felt like this before in his entire adult life. Well, not since Sandy, and he had still been a kid then.

A fierce determination to protect Anais gripped him. He glanced down at her, with her hair splayed across his chest, a satiated half smile playing about her lips, even in sleep, and something inside of him—a deep, dormant feeling—stirred. The three of them here together, felt so natural, so right but...shit, she had so much crap to sort out. Besides, as he had just reminded himself, she was desperate for a family, and just the thought of being responsible for bringing other lives into the world scared him shitless. To say nothing of the promise he'd made to himself when Sandy did the dirty on him. Commitment definitely wasn't for him. It always ended in tears and he could do without that sort of pain.

Hunter stared at the shadows dancing across the ceiling and listened to the even tenor of Anais's breathing for a considerable time before he fell asleep.

He awoke with the dawn, hungry and very erect. Anais was still resting her head on his chest, and was still sound asleep. She didn't appear to have moved a muscle the entire night. Lewis was awake, also watching her.

"Let her sleep a bit longer," Hunter mouthed.

Lewis nodded, and slid almost soundlessly from the bed. Hunter gently removed her head from his chest and placed it on her pillow. She moaned in her sleep, turned on her side, and curled into the fetal position. Hunter climbed out of bed and followed Lewis into his room, where they could shower without disturbing Anais.

"We need to talk about her," Lewis said.

"We need to fix her problems with her husband is what we need to do," Hunter replied evasively.

"Don't shut me out, buddy. I need to know what you're thinking."

Hunter was halfway through pulling his pants on. He paused, and looked up at Lewis. "I'm thinking the unthinkable," he said. "And so far I like what I'm thinking, even if it does scare me shitless."

Lewis's grin was broad and infectious. "Miracles do happen," he said, slapping Hunter's shoulder.

"Don't get ahead of yourself. She's desperate to have kids. Not sure I'm ready for that."

"Not all families are as dysfunctional as the one you grew up in."

"Yours was perfect, but they disowned you because you didn't toe the family line." Lewis conceded the point with a shrug. "Not all abuse is physical. Don't tell me it doesn't still hurt."

"Sure it hurts, but I've learned to live with the memory. If we get too hung up on our pasts, it'll stifle us and our parents will have won."

Hunter wasn't ready to talk about it. He hadn't even intended to say as much as he had. He hadn't even wanted to accept that was the way he was thinking, but his mouth ran away with him. "We'll see," he said. "One step at a time."

Hunter went down to start breakfast, and the smell brought Anais down, too.

"Hmm, morning." Adorably disheveled, she pushed her unruly mop of hair away from her eyes and stretched her arms above her head. "You should have woken me before now."

Hunter leaned across the kitchen counter and stole a kiss. "You earned your sleep, darlin'."

She was tense, her appetite gone, and Hunter knew she had to be thinking about the day ahead.

"It'll be okay," he said, covering one of her hands with his. "We'll be right there with you every step of the way."

"I know, it's just…" She shrugged. "I don't know what I would have done without you guys." She looked at them each in turn, her expression somber and sincere. "Whatever happens today, I want you to know how much I appreciate all you've done for me." She paused.

"And I don't just mean tracking Gary down. All the other stuff we've done together has taught me things about myself that I might never have discovered otherwise. It's been enlightening."

Lewis blew her a kiss across the table. "It's been our pleasure, honey."

Hunter stood up, knowing better than to try and force her to eat. "We'll clear these dishes and hit the road. I'm guessing you want this over with, babe."

"No point backing away from the confrontation," she said, looking as though she would love an excuse to do precisely that. Hunter had never seen her act so hesitant before. He already knew that if she wanted something, she went for it, all guns blazing. He could only begin to imagine her emotional turmoil at that moment, and his heart went out to her.

Half an hour later the three of them were in the truck. It would be a short ride, not allowing Anais time to overthink the situation, which Hunter figured was a good thing. They drove through the town of Immokalee, with tourist shops flaunting its Indian history. There was even a casino run by the Seminoles.

"We need to take this next left," Lewis said, "and follow the road for a couple of miles."

Hunter signaled and took the turn.

"How are we gonna play this?" Lewis asked when they had covered half that distance in taut silence.

"We're going to drive right up to the front door, and I'll knock," Anais said, straightening her shoulders, her expression fixed with determination.

"Not a good idea," Hunter replied. "We don't know what he's into, or with whom."

"I don't care. I—"

"According to the map of the place we looked at on Google, there's a long driveway up to the house. We'll hide the truck some place at the start of the drive, then move up on foot and take a look-see first."

"There was a lot of tree cover around the property," Lewis said, "so that should work. You can wait in the truck while we scope the place, babe."

Anais bridled. "Not a chance!"

Hunter rolled his eyes. "How did I know you were going to say that?"

"This is my life going down the toilet. I've had enough of being a victim and have earned the right to be involved."

"We're just trying to keep you safe," Lewis said mildly. "We don't know what Gary's gotten himself into, but he won't answer the door and invite us in for a beer, you can bet the farm on that. There could be danger. There almost certainly will be. We're used to this stuff, you're not."

"I know you're just trying to protect me." Her stance softened, and she touched Lewis's thigh. "But I need to deal with this."

"Okay," Hunter said. "You can come, but you need to stay behind us and do whatever we tell you to."

It was Anais's turn to roll her eyes, and her irreverence lightened the taut atmosphere in the truck. "When don't I?"

"This is it," Lewis said, his eyes glued to the GPS as he signaled right at an almost-concealed turning through heavy woodland. There was no sign to indicate there was a house at the end of the drive, no mail box, no obvious evidence of life. "He sure doesn't want anyone to know he's here."

"Looks that way," Hunter replied.

He drove past and found a place to pull the truck off the road a short distance away where it would be almost impossible to see it from the road. He and Lewis checked the weapons tucked into the waistbands of their jeans, without making it obvious to Anais that they were carrying.

"Right," he said, sharing a grim expression with Lewis. "Let's do this."

The three of them left the truck and hiked through the trees, Hunter in the lead. They moved quietly and cautiously, always on the lookout for booby traps, or anything that might give their presence away. Even frightening a flock of birds into taking flight en masse would be enough to alert someone as cautious as Harrison.

They hadn't gotten far when a twig snapping behind them alerted the guys to the fact they were being trailed. Hunter and Lewis heard it at once. Anais clearly didn't. Hunter raised a finger to his lips, and continued to move slowly forward. When they reached a thick bush they pushed Anais down behind it, out of harm's way. Their anxiety clearly communicated itself and for once she did as she was told.

Lewis and Hunter moved silently to conceal themselves behind a pair of stout trees. Whoever was following them would have to pass between them. Thirty seconds later, a shadowy figure did so. Hunter and Lewis moved together, felled the person and after a brief struggle they had him subdued. They turned him onto his front, expecting it to be Gary.

It was a total stranger.

"I'm military police," he said. "ID in my jacket pocket."

"Major Dixon." Anais emerged from her hiding place and looked down at the hapless major. "How nice to see you again."

"You alone?" Hunter asked.

"Two more men holding back."

"Tell them to stay put."

Dixon muttered a curt command into a throat mike, and remained passive. Even so, Hunter wasn't taking any chances. He patted the guy down and found a handgun. He also found his ID, which confirmed Anais's identification of the man. Hunter allowed him to stand up.

"You have some explaining to do," Hunter said tersely.

"Not here. Let's go back to Immokalee and we'll tell you everything we know."

"But you know nothing about my husband's disappearance," Anais replied sweetly, her jaw so tightly clenched Hunter could only guess at the feelings of betrayal and anger she was attempting to contain. "You told me so repeatedly."

Two more shadowy figures appeared from the trees. They threw Hunter and Lewis threatening looks, but wisely didn't attempt to intervene.

"Let's get back to town," Hunter said, grasping Anais's elbow. "We'd best hear what they have to say before we decide what action to take next."

"What the hell is going on?" Anais demanded to know as Hunter helped her back into the truck, fired up the engine and did a U turn. Another vehicle closed up behind them, containing the major and his cohorts, then overtook them and led the way to the Immokalee Inn.

"Looks like we're about to find out," Hunter replied, patting her hand as he pulled up outside the dreary two-story motel-like structure.

"This way Mrs. Harrison, gentlemen," the major said, opening the door of their truck and standing beside it, as though he expected them to make a run for it.

Major Dixon took them to a standard ground floor room and ushered them inside.

"Perhaps you'd tell me who you are?" he said to Hunter once they were all inside.

Hunter took stock of his surroundings, and didn't respond immediately. Dixon had two other MPs with him, one of them a tough-looking woman. He was angry but not surprised they'd held out on Anais, and wanted to tell them to go fuck themselves. But if they did that, Dixon would be within his rights to detain them. They obviously had something going on here and could argue that Hunter was impeding their investigation. Best to cooperate, then they might get to something approximating the truth.

"We're Griffin and Kyler, SOCOM vets," he replied, reeling off their ranks and dates when they got out.

"I've heard of you guys," one of the MPs said, sounding suitably awed. "You're legendary."

"Thanks, I think." Hunter pulled a wry smile. "Mrs. Harrison asked us for help when she got nowhere with you guys."

"We didn't know that," Dixon replied. "It must have taken you a while to get this far."

Lewis shrugged. "All of two days."

"Two days!" Dixon shared a glance with his subordinates. "I'm impressed."

Hunter wedged a buttock on the window ledge. "Perhaps you'd care to tell us what you're doing here, why you haven't arrested Harrison, and what the fuck's going on?" he suggested in a pleasant tone that implied he was fast running out of patience. Anais leaned against the window beside him and Lewis took up a position of solidarity on her opposite side. "Start with telling us how long you've known Harrison was alive."

"We suspected something was off about his disappearance right away."

"No shit." Hunter sent him a scathing glance. "Let's cut to the chase here, because Mrs. Harrison is keen for an interview with her husband, and time's a-wasting."

"I'm afraid we can't allow that."

"The hell you can't!" Anais pulled herself up to her full height and glowered at the major. "You've been jerking me around for quite long enough, and don't get to tell me what to do."

"How much do you know about Harrison's situation?" Dixon asked, addressing the question to Hunter.

"We suspect he got turned by the Hondurans and is helping them to get drugs into the US. We think that's why he was taken off active duty, because you suspected him but couldn't prove it," Lewis said.

"And by removing him from active duty, you forced him to show his hand," Hunter added. "You wanted him to lead you to whoever in administrative command got him into this, because someone on the inside has to be pulling his strings. Problem is, you didn't expect him to go AWOL and it's taken you a while to find him."

"Whereas Hunter and Lewis managed it in two days," Anais reminded the major with a sarcastic smile.

Dixon sent her a sheepish look. "He's good at covering his tracks."

"You haven't told us why you're so keen to keep us away from him," Lewis said.

"We don't want them spooked."

"Them?" Anais's head jerked up. "Who's them?"

"Err, well, this is awkward. Sorry, Mrs. Harrison, there's no easy way to tell you this. The fact is your husband hooked up with Maria Sanchez, the daughter of the lynchpin of this smuggling racket, about four years ago, during his first tour of Honduras. We think someone here had already picked up on his dissatisfaction with the service after he'd been disciplined twice for incidents he didn't think were his fault. He had been given Maria's name and was supposed to link up with her in a bar. Sanchez's people would check him out and if he passed muster, then a deal would be struck."

"I find that hard to believe."

"You'd be surprised. Our people on the ground in Honduras tell us Maria routinely acted as her father's go-between. What her father didn't know was that she was tired of her life there, and the violence and killings, and needed someone to help her to get away into the States." He paused and sent Anais another sympathetic smile. "They tell us that Maria and your husband lit one another's fires from the word go and he fell in with her suggestion."

"Right place, right time," Lewis muttered.

"So he's had someone else all these years?" Anais said. "I never even suspected."

"Another woman and two children."

Oh, shit. Hunter should have seen that one coming. Anais looked ready to expire from shock. All color drained from her face, her mouth fell open in a startled *'Oh'* and her entire body trembled.

"Is that who's in that house with him now?"

"Yes. Maria is pregnant again. Their third child is due in three months' time."

Hunter tried to throw a comforting arm around Anais's shoulders, but she shook him off and paced the room, fighting tears. He could sense a dozen questions bubbling beneath the surface of her shock, anger and betrayal, but she didn't voice any of them.

"Let's see if I've got this straight," Hunter said. "Maria had the power to turn a dissatisfied SOCOM sergeant and get him to smuggle her into the States, which is what she wanted all along, and yet she still agrees to be part of the drugs trade she wanted to get away from."

Dixon shrugged. "Both existing children were born here. They are technically US citizens. Tonight a final shipment of drugs is coming in to a local airfield. It's Harrison's swan song. The operation has been compromised mainly because of the interest in Harrison that you've stirred up with your questions, Mrs. Harrison. Everyone knew he wasn't dead, but resources being what they are, the search for him had ground to a halt, the case put on the back burner. Your questions just happened to coincide with intelligence from Honduras about this latest big shipment, so the machine clicked into action and led us to Harrison, by luck rather than intelligent reasoning, I'm sad to admit."

"No wonder they tried to warn you off," Hunter said to Anais.

"Our people tell us this will be the biggest shipment of all tonight. Harrison's contact in admin will be here to get paid off, and we'll get all of them in one hit. That's why you can't go charging in there now, ma'am. You can talk to your husband as much as you like once he's in custody."

"That's incredibly decent of you."

"We want to be there when you take them down," Hunter said.

"I can't allow that."

"You don't have any choice. You have no authority to hold us, and Anais wants to know what this is all about before her husband lawyers up and doesn't say a word."

Dixon thought for a moment, then reluctantly nodded. "Okay, I guess you've earned the right. But you need to stay back until the arrests have gone down."

"Agreed."

Anais slipped her hands into the front pockets of Hunter's jeans and leaned her head against his shoulder. He closed his arms around her and held her close, conscious of her hands burrowing closer and closer to his groin. "This is all too much for me to take in. I need to be alone for a while. Is there somewhere I can lay down?"

"Of course. Sergeant Rourke has a room next door." Dixon snapped his fingers at the female officer. "Rourke, take Mrs. Harrison to your room and stay with her."

"You sure you're all right, babe?" Hunter asked.

She nodded, tears swamping her eyes. "Not really, but I will be. I just need some time."

"Sure. We'll be right here when you're ready to rejoin us." He kissed the top of her head and passed her over to Sergeant Rourke. "Take good care of her now. She's had a shock."

Chapter Fourteen

"Are you all right, Mrs. Harrison?"

Sergeant Rourke placed a hand on Anais's back as she led her next door. It was all Anais could do not to shake it off. Of all the damned fool questions. Of course she wasn't all right. Of all the things she had steeled herself to learn, discovering that Gary was a doting father had certainly not featured, and the knowledge cut into her heart like a dagger.

"Fine."

Anais's shock and anger gradually gave way to a slow fulminating anger, causing her limbs to tremble and tears to gather in her eyes. She was damned if she would let them fall. She was done shedding tears over the two-timing traitor she had married with such optimism in a previous life. Of all the two-faced, double-dealing, disloyal bastards! She had put up with all Gary's moods, making excuses for him, delaying what she wanted more than anything, which was a baby of her own, because she put his welfare ahead of her own needs. Argh! How could she have been such an idiot?

And as for Major Dixon. He had been keeping her in the dark the entire time, not caring about her feelings. He hadn't even bothered to warn her about the raid tonight and give her a chance to prepare. Well, two could play at that game, and she didn't care if she messed up his damned drug capture. She needed to speak to Gary, to make him explain what she had done to deserve such a cruel betrayal, and that conversation was long overdue. He knew…they had talked about her desperate need to have a family so often, and she thought he understood how incomplete she felt as her biological clock kept ticking but her womb remained empty.

Not only had he left her hanging, but he was the one who raided her apartment, trying to scare the shit out of her. Well, Anais had news for her ex-nearest-and-dearest. She was no longer the wilting violet who did everything he asked of her, and it would take more than a scrawled message on a mirror to scare her off. She was going right back to that house to have it out with him, but in order to do that she needed to get rid of Sergeant Rourke. She had assumed she would let her into this room, then leave her be. Instead she had settled into an armchair with a magazine, and didn't look like she planned to move any time soon.

"Have you got everything you need, Mrs. Harrison?" she asked politely.

A gun so I can blast the spineless bastard's head off would be useful.

"Actually, I know this sounds crazy, but whenever I get this wound up, I need chocolate."

"Not crazy at all." Rourke smiled at her. "Ask me, chocolate is every woman's fundamental right in times of crisis."

"I saw a bakery across the road. Can we go over there so I can choose a cake?"

"Why don't you tell me what you need, and I'll go get it for you?"

Thank you! Anais had been counting on the good sergeant wanting to keep her out of sight, just in case Gary should happen to come into town.

"Okay, if you don't mind. Something with lots of chocolate and lashings of cream would hit the spot. I didn't get any breakfast this morning."

Sergeant Rourke grabbed her purse. "I'll be right back."

The door slammed locked behind her. Anais was almost tempted to smile. They were on the ground floor for goodness sake, with a perfectly serviceable opening window. Anais waited until she saw

Rourke disappear around the corner. The only bakery was at the other end of Main Street, at least a couple of minutes' walk away. Hopefully there would be a line.

When the coast was clear she pushed open the window and nimbly climbed through it. Not bothering to close it again, she jogged across to where Hunter had parked his truck, pulled the keys she'd swiped from the front pocket of his jeans from her own pocket and unlocked the vehicle. Thirty seconds later she gunned the engine and burned rubber as she tore out of the lot and sped off in the direction of Gary's love nest. She reckoned she had five minutes tops before she was missed, and intended to make every one of them count.

* * * *

Hunter was worried about Anais, aware that she'd just received a major body blow. Knowing just how anxious she was to have children, and how she had only delayed getting pregnant out of deference to Gary's needs, made his heart break for her. No wonder she needed time to get her head around developments. Hunter wished he could have stayed with her, and comforted her. He glanced at Lewis, restlessly pacing the room, and knew his thoughts were similarly occupied.

"How did you know we were there, just as a matter of interest?" he asked Dixon.

"We have several people posted around the area. You were seen parking up, Mrs. Harrison was recognized, so we had to rush in and stop you trampling all over our sting."

Hunter refrained from using the words that sprang to his lips. "Who do you like as Harrison's inside man?" he asked instead.

"It can only be one of two people, both on the CO's admin staff." Dixon curled his upper lip. "We'll know in a few hours' time. The guy must realize the net's closing in. In fact, we made sure both suspects got to hear about it unofficially. He will be here to collect his cut tonight, and then plans to disappear, just like Harrison did. Unfortunately for him, we'll be here to spoil the party."

"Quite a feather in your cap, Dixon," Lewis remarked.

"That's not what this is about. People like Harrison give the majority of dedicated, hard-working military personnel who risk their lives for their country a bad name."

Hunter couldn't argue with that.

"Even so, I—"

They all turned toward the door when it burst open. Sergeant Rourke stood there, looking flustered and embarrassed.

"What is it, Rourke?" Dixon asked.

"It's Mrs. Harrison, sir."

"What about her?" Hunter and Lewis asked together.

"She's gone."

"Gone?" Hunter thundered. "You were there to keep watch on her."

"She asked if she could go out for chocolate." The sergeant looked sheepish. "I said I'd run the errand for her."

Hunter and Lewis exchanged a protracted glance.

"She can't have gone far," Dixon said. "She will want to head for Harrison's, but doesn't have a vehicle."

Hunter had a nasty feeling that she very well might have. He had liked it when, in her moment of torment, she'd put her hands in his pockets. He'd been too intent upon consoling her to read anything into it. Now he had a horrible feeling he knew what she had done. He patted his pockets and his fears were realized.

"Shit, she took the keys to our truck."

"We'll go after her," Dixon said.

"How long did you leave her for?" Lewis asked.

"It must have been seven or eight minutes. There was a line at the bakery."

"Then you'll never catch her," Hunter replied. "I should have read more into her need to rest, damn it!" He thumped his clenched fist against the window sill. "She's put herself in danger."

"To say nothing of our operation," Dixon added.

"Fuck your operation," Hunter and Lewis said together.

"Can't we call one of the men stationed there to cut her off?" Rourke asked.

"She'll be almost there by now."

Sure enough, Dixon's cell phone rang. It was one of his command reporting sight of the truck entering the road at speed.

"Lewis and I will go get her," Hunter said. "If you go then your operation will be compromised."

"It will be anyway if she tells Harrison we're here," Dixon replied.

"I doubt she will. She just needs to talk to him, and try to understand why he did what he did."

"She could have done that after we arrested him."

"We don't have time to argue this now." Hunter held out his hand. "Give me the keys to one of your vehicles and tell you men to let us pass."

Dixon hesitated for a second or two, then handed the keys over. "The black SUV," he said.

"Wise move." Lewis scowled at him. "But you do realize that if you'd leveled with Mrs. Harrison when you first knew her husband was alive, this situation wouldn't have arisen."

And with that the two of them left the room at a run.

* * * *

Anais had absolutely no idea what she planned to say to Gary. All she knew was that she had to confront him. The rational part of her brain told her she was being reckless, but reckless seemed like the right way to go. Despite the promises Dixon had made, she would never get to talk to Gary properly once he'd been arrested. *If* he was arrested. She had a feeling they were underestimating him, and he probably knew he was being watched. He'd outfoxed them all for this long, and it sounded like he had good motivation to carry on doing so. A motivation that came in the form of a fully-fledged family.

Renewed anger surged through her as she took the turn toward Gary's house on two wheels, not caring if she was giving him advance notice of her arrival. Sure that she would be. She stood on the brakes, sending a shower of gravel into the air when she stopped outside the front stoop. She climbed from the truck, leaving the door hanging open, and ascended the stairs.

"You never did learn to leave well alone, did you, sugar?" said her husband's voice.

She looked up at him, and at the rifle held in rock-steady hands, and sent him a look of pure vitriol that appeared to take him aback. He had probably expected tears, demands for an explanation, histrionics even. Instead she was holding him in a death glare.

"I need to know why," she replied simply. "Oh, don't worry, I don't want you back. In fact I wouldn't touch you with a barge pole."

"How did you find me?"

"I asked first."

"And I'm the one with the rifle."

"Which you won't use on me."

"You sound pretty damned sure of yourself, so let me guess. You got some private dicks to go asking all sorts of questions, and managed to piece it all together. That jag in your apartment with Regan was a setup." He chuckled. "Looks like I underestimated you."

"Don't feel bad. It's not the first time."

He abruptly stopped chuckling and frowned instead. "There's something different about you."

"You pull a clumsy disappearing act on me, leave me hanging, and wonder why I've changed."

"Yeah, sorry about that. I didn't plan to bail quite so soon, but the bloodhounds were getting suspicious, asking awkward questions, so I had no choice. Given more time I could have made a much better job of it."

"You still haven't told me why," she said, acting ignorant about his woman and kids, a small part of her still hoping it wasn't true. She didn't care about the woman—she was welcome to Gary—but the children bit hurt like crazy.

As if on cue, the door to the house opened and one of the most beautiful women Anais had ever seen walked through it, a toddler perched on her hip. Anais gasped, unable to look away. The woman had thick black hair that shone like a raven's wing and hung halfway to her waist. She had lovely features, flashing brown eyes, and was still elegant and statuesque even with a belly swollen from pregnancy. The child had curly black hair and equally large eyes that were fastened in fascination upon Anais. Obviously, strangers were a rarity around these parts.

"Does that answer your question?"

"Who is this?" the woman asked at the same time.

"Maria, meet Anais," Gary said casually. "Anais, Maria."

"Your wife?" Maria's already large eyes almost doubled in size. "*Diablo!* What is she doing here?"

"It's okay, baby. She came alone."

"No I didn't."

"Go back inside, Maria. I've got it covered, but Serena doesn't need to see it."

"Be careful. It might be a trap."

"It's no trap. I'll know if anyone else breaks the perimeter, just like I knew she was coming when she got halfway down the drive."

"Now perhaps you understand why," Gary said smugly.

"She's very beautiful." Anais gulped. "So is the baby, but I didn't realize you were so dissatisfied with our marriage."

"We lost what we'd once had, darlin', you know that as well as I do. It's nobody's fault, except perhaps the army's. People change as they grow older, and want different things."

"Not so very different," she replied, nodding towards Maria's retreating figure.

"Ah, that old refrain. *When can we think about a baby, Gary?* But there was no way I'd agree, because I knew we wouldn't be together much longer, even before I met Maria. No way would I let my child be raised just by its mother. Kids need a man, discipline, in their lives. Then I met Maria, and my priorities changed. No offense."

"None taken." Anais shrugged. "Why couldn't you just have asked me for a divorce? I would have given you one."

"I doubt that very much. You were stifling me, Anais, but just couldn't see it. You are so fucking naïve."

His tone chilled her, but she didn't allow it to show, and responded with a secretive smile. "Not anymore."

"Yeah, you've had to grow up, I can see that, but this is about me, not you." *Oh really?* "I had gotten too big for the army. Its restrictions were stifling me every bit as much as you were." He turned his head to one side and spat on the boarded verandah, but the rifle didn't waiver. "Way too many dumb rules. You can't corral a man with my talents. Talents, I might add, that went unappreciated and unrecognized. I even got disciplined for using my initiative." He rolled his eyes. "The army doesn't value a man of experience who can think for himself and do a better job of it than the officers who are paid to do the thinking."

"That must have been so frustrating," Anais said sarcastically.

"You have no idea. Anyway, Maria ain't the type of lady who can live on fresh air."

"I don't want to hear this."

Anais realized now just how stupid she had been to come. Had she really expected Gary to do anything other than make half-ass excuses, blaming everyone except himself for what he'd done? And he couldn't let her go again. In her anger and righteous indignation she hadn't stopped to think it through properly, assuming even he wouldn't do away with his own wife. She could see from the glacial set to his features that she had severely underestimated his determination to make a fresh start.

"It don't matter none that you know. After tonight we'll be long gone. No one knows for sure I'm still alive."

"But what about me?"

"What indeed?" He shook his head. "You really should have listened when I tried to warn you off."

* * * *

Hunter and Lewis reached the perimeter of Gary's land, where they were met by one of Dixon's men who had been ordered to brief them.

"You can get to within five hundred feet of the house," they were told. "Then there are all sorts of traps that'll warn Harrison you've come calling."

"What sort of traps?" Hunter asked.

"Oh, the usual survival shit. Pits, trip wires, saplings that'll spring up and set bells ringing, literally."

"Okay, we can deal with that." Hunter thanked the man. "You ready to go get our lady, buddy?"

"You'd better believe it."

"We'll stay back beyond the five-hundred-feet mark," the MP said. "If you're not out within fifteen minutes, we have orders to blow the operation and come get you."

"Don't!" Hunter said sternly. "You could risk the woman's life. Leave it to us."

"I can't disobey a direct order."

"I don't have time for this. Just leave it to us. We know what we're doing. Keep in touch by text."

"Okay, that'll work."

"Dixon must have had a fit of conscience since we left him," Lewis said as they set off through the trees.

"More like he doesn't want to face the consequences if a civilian gets killed in the crossfire," Hunter replied with a cynical snort. "Okay, we're getting close. You know what to look for."

They found and bypassed several of Gary's traps, but almost fell into a third. Hunter saw it at the eleventh hour and pulled Lewis back before he could walk into it.

"Thanks," Lewis said softly. "I got sloppy for a moment."

They could now see the house, and crouched behind a line of bushes.

"Shit, they're on the verandah and he's got a gun on her." Hunter's heart lurched as he watched the woman he loved so recklessly risk her life. He was filled with rage against Gary, feeling impotent because there was absolutely nothing he could do without putting her in further danger. "What a slime ball."

"Can we get a clear shot at him from here?" Lewis asked.

Hunter shook his head. "Not without risking hitting Anais. We don't have rifles."

"Fuck!"

"Hang on, something's happening."

Hunter swore as he watched Gary Harrison bind his wife's hands behind her back. He lifted a trapdoor in the verandah floor that presumably led to some sort of crawl space and pushed Anais hard so she fell into it. He said something to her and then slammed the heavy door closed.

"At least he didn't shoot her," Lewis said.

"Not yet, but he can't afford any loose ends."

"Why not? If he's planning to haul out tonight, what difference does it make?"

"She presumably knows about the women and kids. Harrison won't take any chances about them being found, or him. Look."

They watched as a pregnant woman and a child came out of the house. Harrison followed carrying a baby, then went back for a couple of bags. He loaded family and belongings into the truck Lewis had seen him in at the beach and looked ready to climb behind the wheel.

"He's moving out now," Hunter said.

"Probably worried this place has been compromised. He must think Anais didn't find him on his own."

"What's he doing now?" Lewis asked.

Both men watched in growing concern. "Shit, he's setting charges," Hunter said, appalled. "The whole fucking place is gonna blow with Anais inside it."

* * * *

Anais was petrified of confined spaces. This one was too small for her to be able to stand upright. It also smelt of damp, and was full of crawly things. She could feel something biting her legs, which freaked her out. But not nearly as badly as the dead look in Gary's eyes when be pushed her down here, telling her to make her peace with her god. She told him the army knew about his hideout, but he just laughed and said it didn't matter. There would soon be nothing left of it for them to find.

Shit, she had been an impulsive fool! He had gleefully told her that the whole house would explode once it got dark, after he'd taken care of his business elsewhere and gotten well clear of the area. He seemed keen for her to know he had planned to do that all along. Couldn't afford to leave any trace evidence if he wanted to make a new start, apparently. The idiot seemed to think she should sympathize about his differences of opinion with the army, and understand why he'd been forced to do what he was doing. But until he pushed her into the crawl space, she really didn't think he would go so far as to kill her.

Now she knew better.

The man she had once loved had turned into a coldhearted killing machine, with no conscience, putting the blame on her for the situation she found herself in because she hadn't stopped looking for answers. She thought that made him psychotic, a sociopath, or something like that. She didn't know the correct term for his mental state, nor did it matter much. She had more immediate concerns.

She was an idiot, she told herself, pulling futilely at the rope binding her hands. It dug into her wrists, but didn't budge. Gary was far too good at tying knots to allow her any wiggle room. What the hell was she supposed to do now? She would have been missed and Hunter and Lewis would come looking for her. But they would find the house empty, and never think to look down here. Even if they did, Gary had mentioned that touching the door would set off the charge and they would be killed, too.

Damn, she loved them both like crazy, and would never get to tell them how she felt. It was so unfair. She wanted to scream with frustration—at herself, mostly, for being so stupid—but also because she would very likely get Hunter and Lewis killed. Gary had relieved her of her cell phone, but even if he hadn't, she couldn't have used it with her hands tied behind her. Anyway, she would never get a signal down here.

Refusing to accept defeat when she had finally discovered the true meaning of love and had something to live for, she squirmed about on the damp earth. She ignored the various creepy things crawling over her exposed skin, and eventually managed to push her feet over her bonds so her hands finished up in front of her. They were still securely tied, but this small victory gave her fresh hope.

"I'm not done yet, you cowardly bastard!" she shouted at the top of her lungs, just so she could hear her own voice.

She crawled about on her hands and knees, looking for something, anything, to help her get her hands untied. If she could manage that, she would feel around for the hatch opening and try to pry it loose. She didn't care if it exploded. Well, she did. Of course she did. But better she was blown to smithereens than Hunter and Lewis went with her.

She found a sharply pointed rock and cried out in triumph. Grasping it awkwardly between her numb, bleeding fingers, she started the laborious business of sawing it through the rope.

* * * *

Hunter and Lewis waited for the truck to disappear, then swung into action. They called Dixon to update him, and he set his men in motion to follow Harrison's truck in a series of different vehicles.

"We have a pretty good idea where he's headed. There are only two places locally where a small plane can land. He won't get away."

"We don't give a shit about him. Anais is in the crawl space and the whole place is set to blow. We need to get her out."

"Wait. I'll call for bomb disposal."

"How long before they can get here?"

"Hold on. I'll find out." Hunter heard orders being issued, then Dixon came back on the line. "They are two hours out."

"Can't wait that long. This baby's set to blow in just over an hour, according to this ticking clock here. We'll have deal with it ourselves."

"Do you know what you're doing?"

Hunter's jaw clenched, square and unmoving. "Only one way to find out."

Hunter cut the call and he and Lewis jogged over to the property, guns drawn. They didn't think there was anyone else left there, apart from Anais, but they weren't taking any chances. Once they ensured the place was clear Lewis, who knew more about explosives than Hunter did, crouched down on the verandah where they had seen Gary setting the charges.

"It's timed to go off later tonight, but it's pretty damned crude. Any vibration could set it off before then." Lewis emitted a mirthless chuckle. "We've found something Harrison isn't proficient at."

"Can you disarm it?" Hunter asked.

"I think so."

"I need to check on Anais." Hunter went to lift the hatch.

"Wait! It might be triggered to blow if lifted."

Several agonizing minutes went past while Lewis fiddled with the intricate workings of the homemade incendiary device. Hunter wanted to call out to Anais, but didn't for fear she might try to open the hatch from her side.

"Okay," Lewis said, his voice terse. "I'm as sure as I can be that if I cut this wire…you might wanna stand back, buddy, just in case."

"Not a chance." Hunter slapped Lewis's shoulder. "I have complete faith in your abilities."

"Well, that makes one of us." Lewis paused to wipe perspiration from his brow. "Right, here goes."

The two guys shared a protracted look, then Lewis cut the wire, and they both tensed, waiting for the place to blow.

Nothing happened.

"Shit, you did it, bud." Hunter exhaled with relief and shared a high five with Lewis. "Way to go!"

"No need to sound so surprised."

Hunter laughed as he turned the heavy handle and lifted the hatch to the crawl space. "You down there, babe?"

"No! Get clear." Anais sounded frantic. "It's going to explode."

"No, it's not. Lewis defused it." Hunter reached a hand down and took both of hers, tied with a frayed rope, in his. He pulled her up and into his arms. "You okay?"

"I am now that you're here." She was covered in dirt and sobbing. "I'm so sorry. I was stupid, and I spooked Gary into running."

"Dixon's on him," Lewis said, taking his turn for a hug.

"Look at your poor wrists," Hunter said, tutting as he unfastened the rope and saw they were dripping with blood.

"I was trying to get my hands free so I could open the hatch."

"And kill yourself?" the guys asked together.

"Better than you getting killed trying to rescue me," she replied, fresh tears cutting a path through the dirt on her face.

Chapter Fifteen

Hunter swept her into his arms and carried her into the house. Lewis found a bowl, which he filled with warm water. He bathed her wrists and tenderly bandaged them while Hunter cleaned the rest of the dirt from her as best he could. Then he called Dixon to update him on the situation.

"We're invited to watch your husband being arrested when the drug deal goes down," he said to Anais. "Wanna be there?"

"Bet your life I do," she said, showing a return of her old spirit.

Hunter laughed, conveyed Anais's wishes to Dixon, and ushered her out to the truck. "We're to leave Dixon's vehicle. One of his men will pick it up. We're to rendezvous with Dixon outside of town."

"Glad to see you in one piece, Mrs. Harrison," Dixon said when they arrived. "Maria and the children are in a motel about a mile away. They will be picked up after we have Gary and his accomplice."

"How long do we have to wait?" Lewis asked.

"Shouldn't be much longer now," Dixon replied as darkness fell. "We'll get a call when we know where they're at, and move in on them."

Hunter wondered if the drop would be aborted. Gary must wonder if the operation had been compromised because he would know Anais hadn't found him without help.

"We're on," Dixon said tersely a short time later when he received a call.

"Greed won out over common sense," Hunter muttered.

"Harrison is heading along a dirt track to a small isolated airfield. So is another vehicle."

"Do you know who's in it?" Hunter asked before heading for his truck.

"Not yet. This place is very isolated. I already have people posted out of sight around it, ready to close in. We will have to stop short and hike in. Any vehicles will be seen, and there's little tree cover. You need to stay in the truck, ma'am."

"Of course," Anais said sweetly.

Hunter bit back a laugh. There was about as much chance of her doing that as there was of Hunter winning the lottery—and he didn't play it. But she'd wised up since her impulsive headlong flight into her husband's murderous path and presumably understood Dixon would stop her from tagging along if she didn't agree to his terms.

"They chose this place well," Lewis said, glancing through night vision goggles supplied by Dixon at the isolated dirt strip. They'll see us immediately if we get any closer. Anais was with them. Dixon had either forgotten about her staying in the truck, or had decided it was pointless trying to force her.

"Don't worry," Dixon replied, pointing to a couple of quad bikes that had been pushed by MPs up to their position. "There are more of these with the guys surrounding the place. They won't get away."

Hunter laughed. All the high-tech equipment available to the modern army and these guys would be taken down by MPs on quad bikes. Go figure. They watched as temporary landing lights were set out on the dirt strip. The tension was palpable when the sound of a light aircraft's engine reached their ears.

"Stand by," Dixon said tersely into his radio.

Without its lights on, the aircraft made a rocky landing and rolled to a halt. Harrison and his buddy sprang forward. The pilot climbed from the cockpit, stood on the wing, and started throwing packages to Harrison.

"Go, go, go!"

Blinding lights illuminated the aircraft from all four corners of the field, effectively blocking it on the makeshift runway. Quad bikes closed in at speed.

"Raise your hands," Dixon called through a bullhorn. "You are surrounded."

Hunter knew it wouldn't end well, even when Harrison's hands went up in the air. He knew what fate awaited him, and wouldn't give up without a fight. It was too easy.

"That's Bains with him," Dixon said, peering through his goggles and sighing. "Shit, I was hoping it wouldn't be him. He's been the CO's adjutant for years. Christ knows what other operations he's compromised. He'll have a lot of questions to answer."

Hunter kept his eyes glued to the scene going down. The quad bikes had reached Harrison, Bains, and the pilot. The soldiers left the vehicles and a dozen rifles were trained upon the criminals. Perhaps it would be all right after all, but Hunter still had a bad feeling. One of the MPs went to cuff Harrison, which is when it all went tits up. It happened so fast that Hunter had no clear idea of what actually did happen. One minute Harrison was being cuffed. The next the MP cuffing him was laying on the ground with a bullet hole through his forehead. Before anyone could react, Harrison took one of the quad bikes and was speeding away.

"Shit, kill those fucking lights!" Dixon bellowed.

It would make no difference to Harrison, Hunter thought. In fact, it would be an advantage. He knew the area well, and would get clean away. The MPs were fussing over their dead colleague and making sure Bains and the pilot were secure. No one had taken off after Harrison, and Hunter wasn't prepared to allow him to escape. He grabbed one of the quad bikes, fired up the engine, pulled his night vision goggles into place and roared off after him.

"Hunter, no!" Anais's anguished cry barely registered. "Let him go. It's not our problem."

Hunter was back in combat mode, focused and determined. Harrison would kill him without a second thought. He was clever, resourceful and desperate—a lethal combination. But Hunter was equally determined. He hadn't forgotten the look on Anais's face when she came out of that crawl hole, he hadn't forgotten the damage to her wrists, or any aspect of the ordeal she had suffered at the hands of the man he was now pursuing—a man who had once loved her.

Hunter opened up the throttle and closed the distance between himself and his quarry. He had an advantage because of the night vision goggles that cast the world green, and clearly showed him the direction Harrison was taking. Harrison was an expert shot but even he couldn't fire accurately over his shoulder while trying to negotiate rugged terrain in the pitch dark. A shot whistled past his ear, so close that he felt a draft as it missed his ear by a whisker, forcing him to reevaluate. Fuck, that was close.

Hunter tucked himself lower over the handlebars, presenting a smaller target but not letting up with the chase. The terrain was uneven. Soft in places, littered with rocks in others, and the bike was constantly thrown off course. It took all Hunter's concentration to keep it upright, but then the same must be true for Harrison.

He heard another bike following behind him, and knew Lewis had his back, just like always. He gave a hand signal and the two of them, at full throttle, separated. Each had one of Harrison's flanks, making it harder for him to get a shot off. He was losing ground and needed to concentrate on staying ahead of them. Hunter saw him glance over his shoulder and raise his gun. He had Hunter in his direct line of sight, and Hunter was moving too fast to get out of the way. He lifted his own weapon, and aimed for Harrison's tires. He knew without having to look that Lewis would be doing the same thing.

Harrison's gun fired and Hunter felt a searing pain in his shoulder. He had no choice but to slow his bike. At the exact same time, Harrison's bike flew in the air, sending its rider tumbling to the ground in a crashing fall. Either they had hit its tires, or the bike had hit a rut at speed and Harrison had lost control. Hunter stopped his own machine, grabbed his shoulder to stem the flow of blood and walked with Lewis over to where Harrison lay on the ground, not moving. Lewis kicked him and he groaned.

"You okay, bud?" Lewis asked, glancing at the blood seeping between Hunter's fingers.

"Just a flesh wound, I think."

Dixon pulled up in a Jeep, by which time a bleeding and defeated Harrison was sitting up, clutching his head and swearing up a storm. He was cuffed, none too gently, and thrown in the back of the Jeep. A medic stepped forward to attend to Hunter but Hunter waved him away.

"It's okay."

The airstrip was again flooded with light when they returned to it. Anais ran forward and threw her arms around Hunter.

"You're hurt!"

"It's nothing, babe."

Gary watched them, his expression dumbfounded, as Anais kissed them. "Both of them?" His lips twitched. "Seems I really did underestimate you. I thought you were strictly a missionary position type of gal."

"Whose fault would that be?" Anais replied sweetly. "Who taught me everything I knew about sex." She turned to Hunter and Lewis, placing a hand in each of theirs. "Until recently."

Gary shook his head. "I'll be damned."

"Very likely." She sent Gary a scathing look, before turning to Hunter with a concerned smile. "Let's get that shoulder seen to, then you can take me home. We're all done here."

Chapter Sixteen

Anais felt safe and secure, sandwiched between her guys, as they drove her home.

"Dixon needs to debrief you, darlin', but I told him to go fuck himself," Hunter said.

"I'll talk to him tomorrow." She smiled at them, feeling as though a huge weight had been lifted from her shoulders. Without being aware of it before now, she had lived for years thinking she had somehow let Gary down, not supported him when he needed it the most, and so anything he did wrong had to have been partly her fault. Now she knew better, and the only thing she regretted was putting Hunter and Lewis at risk with her impulsive action. "I'm so sorry I endangered you both," she said. "I'll never forgive myself for that."

"You did what you had to do."

Hunter's voice was terse, distant. Anais assumed he must be in a lot of pain now that the adrenaline had worn off, but knew he would never admit it. Lewis was equally quiet as he concentrated on the road, ignoring the speed limit. Anais had so many questions, so much she wanted to say to them both, but it was late and all three of them were beat.

When they got home she headed straight for her room, and a hot shower. She half hoped they would follow her, but wasn't surprised when they didn't. It was obvious she wouldn't be invited to share Hunter's bed for a second night. That was okay. Well, actually it wasn't. Her heart was breaking at the prospect of leaving them, but she knew it was what she had to do. They were making it crystal clear by keeping their distance that she was in danger of overstaying her welcome. It would be a miracle if she wasn't, given that she'd endangered their lives twice today.

She still felt her insides quail every time she recalled watching the quad bike chase through the night vision goggles she had grabbed from one of Dixon's men. She saw the bright flash of bullets and died a little inside, knowing Gary would almost certainly kill one of her men, if not both of them. He was too good a shot not to, even though he was disadvantaged. That they both came through, virtually unscathed, seemed like nothing short of a miracle.

Anais slept late, but there was no welcoming smell of bacon frying to lure her downstairs. She went down anyway and found the kitchen and den devoid of human presence. She heard voices coming from the study, which was where they had to be. She didn't go in search of them but flipped the kettle on instead, in urgent need of coffee. They both appeared just as it was ready.

"How's your shoulder?" she asked Hunter anxiously.

"It's fine. How about your wrists?"

"They're good. Now stop being brave, and tell me the truth."

"Really, it's just a bit stiff. It'll mend."

Lewis eyed her speculatively but didn't say a word. Hunter lapsed into silence, too, and the situation was in danger of becoming embarrassing. They definitely wanted her gone. Probably wondered what she was still doing there.

"I'll be gone soon as I've had coffee," she said defensively. "Dixon wants to see me."

"Gone?" Lewis's head snapped in her direction. "Where?"

"Why?" Hunter added.

"Back to my apartment, my life." She shrugged, unable to understand their confusion. "I'm cramping your style here."

"Come and sit down. We need to talk."

Hunter held out a hand, and Anais instinctively slipped hers into it. He sat her in the center of one of the sofas, and the guys took up positions on either side of her, just like always.

"Lewis and I have just been talking about you." Hunter paused and ran a hand through his hair. "The thing is, we don't want you to go."

"Well, I don't want to either, but—"

"We want you to stay with us," Lewis explained. "Permanently."

"You what!" Anais gaped at each of them, her mouth hanging open rather inelegantly. "Did I just hear you right?"

"We love you." Hunter made it sound like it ought to have been obvious to her. "We kinda hoped you might feel the same way about us."

"Well, I do, but I don't see how—"

"Nor did I, at first," Hunter replied. "Commitment scares me shitless, as it does Lewis, and we've always stuck together because that makes it easier to avoid."

"But when the right person comes along to commit to, it's not necessary to fear it." Hunter rested a large hand on her thigh. "You've taught me that."

"Shit, Anais, when we saw Gary push you into that crawl space and realized it was wired up, I thought...well, you don't wanna know what I thought." Lewis placed his hand on her other thigh. "Don't ever frighten us like that again."

"Kids were the stumbling block for me," Hunter added. "I know how much you want them, but I've never wanted the responsibility. After the shit I had to put up with when I was young, I wasn't prepared to take the chance."

"Me neither." Lewis grinned at her. "But for you we're willing to have a change of heart."

Anais wanted to pinch herself. She was convinced she must have misheard them. "You are?" Jeez, instead of being the happiest woman on earth, she sounded like a moron, unable to string an intelligible sentence together.

"Yep," Hunter replied, grinning. "We are. And as it happens, we're pretty sure we know how to make them."

Anais laughed aloud. "I'm absolutely sure you do."

"Marry one of us, babe," Hunter begged. "Just as soon as you've divorced that jerk, of course. It doesn't matter which one. You'll be ours to love and to share for the rest of our lives, if you'll say *yes*."

"Yes!" she cried, tears streaming down her face as she threw her arms around Lewis, and then more cautiously around Hunter, careful to avoid his injury. "Yes. Yes, please. Yes, I love you both. Yes, yes, yes!"

"Was that a *yes?*" Hunter asked with a devastating smile as he leaned in for a kiss.

* * * *

"The good guys strike again," Raoul said, punching the air as he hung up the speakerphone, having just received a full debrief on the Harrison situation from Hunter and Lewis.

"Harrison isn't the first killing machine made by the army to turn against it, and almost certainly won't be the last."

"Interesting that he insists the Sanchez woman knew nothing about his activities, and wasn't involved. He's taking the wrap, telling them everything in return for her being left alone and allowed to remain in the US. He doesn't want her father to get control of her and his kids."

Zeke shrugged. "Ain't love grand."

"Talking of which, we're not taking any more cases if the client's an attractive woman."

Zeke chuckled. "You're just pissed because Hunter and Lewis have hooked up permanently with Anais."

"Fucking right I am." Raoul scowled at the opposite wall. "That's the fourth time recently that we've lost a couple of decent operatives to a client. That's no way to repay us."

"You need to get back up onto the horse, buddy, before cynicism turns you bitter."

"Me, a cynic?" Raoul flashed a wry grin. "I think you've got the wrong guy."

"Come on, let's go into town, get a beer, and find some action."

"Nah, I've got stuff to do."

"Raoul, it's time you became a serious player again," Zeke said. "Cantara wouldn't want you to stop living, just because—"

"Just because she's dead?"

"Yeah. She knew the risks when she agreed to work with the Americans, and if she could see the way you've been acting ever since she passed she'd have your balls."

"They're hers anyway," Raoul said bleakly. "Besides, she wouldn't be dead if we'd gone in quicker to save her."

"You have got to stop beating yourself up, man. The operation was blown, and she was dead before we got anywhere near, and we fucking near died ourselves. End of." Zeke picked up Raoul's jacket and threw it at him. "Come on, don't make me hurt you."

Raoul snapped out of his self-pitying mood and grabbed the keys to their truck. "Oh, for fuck's sake. If that's what it will take to keep you quiet."

Zeke slapped Raoul's shoulder and grinned. "Fuck's sake about covers it."

THE END

WWW.ZARACHASE.COM

ABOUT THE AUTHOR

Zara Chase is a British author who spends a lot of her time travelling the world. Being a gypsy provides her with ample opportunities to scope out exotic locations for her stories. She likes to involve the heroines in her erotic novels in all sorts of dangerous situations—and not only with the hunky heroes whom they encounter along the way. Murder, blackmail, kidnapping, and fraud—to name just a few of life's more common crimes—make frequent appearances in her books, adding pace and excitement to her racy stories.

Zara is an animal lover who enjoys keeping fit and is on a one-woman mission to keep the wine industry ahead of the recession.

For all titles by Zara Chase, please visit
www.bookstrand.com/zara-chase

Siren Publishing, Inc.
www.SirenPublishing.com

CPSIA information can be obtained at www.ICGtesting.com
Printed in the USA
LVOW04s1043140415

434402LV00036B/2062/P